Reade[illegible] ABANDON . . .

'Tristan and Senia are on fire, their chemistry is off the charts and their story is unexpected and simply beautiful'
Natasha is a Book Junkie

'Tristan is AMAZING and sexy as hell. Trust us, you will not regret picking up this book'
Book Obsession 813

'This story is a beautifully written book about facing your past and learning to move forward and live without anger – and it has the perfect amount of hot and sexy times. My heart ached for Tristan and I absolutely loved his story'
The Book Bella

'It takes you on a roller coaster of highs and lows'
Sammie's Book Blog

'Emotional, funny, realistic and heartwarming . . . I adored Tristan!'
Bookhooking

'Cassia will once again instantly pull you in. Her writing always flows perfectly giving you the perfect amount of romance, sexy scenes, humour and swoony moments'
Sarah's Book Blog

'Be ready for a roller coaster of emotions'
Mean Girls Luv Books

'Another emotional and gut wrenching yet beautiful story'
Louise Seraphim Reviews

www.transworldbooks.co.uk

New York Times and *USA Today* bestselling author Cassia Leo loves her coffee, chocolate, and margaritas with salt. When she's not writing, she spends way too much time watching old reruns of *Friends* and *Sex and the City*. When she's not watching reruns, she's usually enjoying the California sunshine or reading – sometimes both. She is the author of the ***Shattered Hearts*** series (*Relentless*, *Pieces of You*, *Bring Me Home*). She is also the author of the hugely popular ***Luke*** and ***Chase*** series, as well as a stand-alone novel, *Black Box*.

Chat with her on Facebook:
www.facebook.com/authorcassialeo or
Twitter: www.twitter.com/AuthorCassiaLeo

Or you can follow her blog at www.cassialeo.com to stay up-to-date on new releases and giveaways.

Thanks for reading!

By Cassia Leo

ABANDON
BLACK BOX

The Shattered Hearts series

RELENTLESS
PIECES OF YOU
BRING ME HOME

ABANDON

Cassia Leo

CORGI BOOKS

TRANSWORLD PUBLISHERS
61–63 Uxbridge Road, London W5 5SA
www.transworldbooks.co.uk

Transworld is part of the Penguin Random House group of companies
whose addresses can be found at global.penguinrandomhouse.com

First published in Great Britain
in 2014 by Transworld Digital
an imprint of Transworld Publishers
Corgi edition published 2015

A CIP catalogue record for this book
is available from the British Library.

ISBN
9780552171113

Typeset in 12/15pt Adobe Caslon by Kestrel Data, Exeter, Devon.
Printed and bound by Clays Ltd, St Ives plc

Penguin Random House is committed to a sustainable future for
our business, our readers and our planet. This book is made
from Forest Stewardship Council® certified paper.

1 3 5 7 9 10 8 6 4 2

For all the Tristans
I've ever known.

Chapter One

She walks into Yogurtland with her cell phone pressed to her ear and a scowl on her face. Behind the scowl, her vulnerability shines like a fucking nuclear explosion in a dark closet. Whoever she's talking to has stripped her bare. I find myself wishing it were me who affected her that way.

She's digging inside her purse while balancing the phone between her shoulder and her ear; probably searching for money to get her frozen yogurt fix. What is it about frozen yogurt that makes us feel better? Maybe it reminds us of being kids, and how something as simple as a trip to the yogurt shop could turn a bad day into a great one. Whatever it is, I can see that she desperately needs her fix. But with each passing moment that she's unable to locate her money, I see the hope draining from her face.

'I told you to stop calling me. I don't care if your car is in the shop. I'm not picking you up!'

She drops her purse and cell phone onto the

checkered tile floor and curses loudly. 'What the fuck are you staring at?' she barks at the man who's ogling her ass while ushering his small child out of the shop. 'You've never seen a girl in a skirt bend over?'

She falls to her knees as she reaches for the cell phone. She presses it to her ear and says hello a few times before she realizes there's no one there. I walk over to her, coolly taking my time, then I kneel next to her and reach for the lipstick tube that rolled behind her left foot. I hold it out in front of her. She looks sideways at me and her mouth drops as she's stunned into silence. Most girls are stunned when they see me. I'm used to that. But Senia has seen me plenty of times. She's not amazed by my good looks. She's stupefied by my impeccable timing.

Her gaze immediately falls to my lips, which are just inches from her own. Then she begins to sob as she drops her purse and throws her arms around my neck.

I can't help but chuckle. 'Hey, it's okay,' I whisper into her ear, breathing in her scent. She smells like strawberries or pineapple. Something fruity. It's intoxicating.

I reach up and grab her face to pull her away, so I can look her in the eye. 'What flavor do you want?'

A tear rolls down her face and I wipe it away as she stares at me, still dumbfounded. 'Cheesecake, with strawberries.'

'Perfect.'

I help her gather the rest of her belongings into

her purse then I order her yogurt as she watches me from where she stands next to the trash bin. Her gaze follows me as I approach her with her bowl, one of her perfect eyebrows cocked skeptically.

'Don't look at me like that,' I say as I pass her the bowl of yogurt.

'Why?' she says and she pops the first spoon into her mouth.

She licks the spoon clean and I find myself wondering what it would feel like to have those full, red lips wrapped around my cock. I lean in and whisper in her ear, 'Because you're turning me on and I can't fuck you in Yogurtland.'

She continues to cock her eyebrow as she takes another spoonful of creamy yogurt into her mouth. 'Then maybe we should get the fuck out of Yogurtland.'

In the three years I've known Senia, we've almost fucked three times. The first time happened the day I met her, after a show we played in Durham. We were interrupted backstage by Xander, the band's manager, just as Senia was about to get on her knees. The second time was at a Memorial Day picnic. We were both pretty shit-faced and she ended up tossing her cookies all over me as I was sliding her panties off. The third time was less than three months ago, in a pub restroom stall. She started crying and couldn't go through with it; she was too heartbroken over her ex. I think the fourth time may be the charm for us. For some reason, this makes me really fucking nervous.

I'm not afraid I won't be able to satisfy her. There's no doubt I'll make her come harder than she's ever come before. But for the first time in my life, I'm afraid of what will happen after the sex.

Senia is Claire's best friend. And Chris is my best friend. Once upon a time, Claire and Chris were the golden couple; everyone assumed they'd be together forever. Then they broke up before we went on tour last year. They've spent the last few months attempting to reconcile the issues caused by their breakup. Even if Claire and Chris never get back together, I know Claire will always be around. I can't avoid Claire and, therefore, I can't avoid Senia. Something about this terrifies me and intrigues me – like I'm flirting with danger or, more accurately, fucking with danger.

I grab the door handle on the passenger side of my silver Lightning and pause as I look her in the eye and pull the door open. 'Get in.'

She smiles and shakes her head as she slinks into the passenger seat. 'Please don't bother using your manners.'

'I won't.'

I slam the door shut and walk around to the driver's side, tapping the trunk as I note my surroundings. It's eight in the evening. There are only three other cars in the parking lot and at least one of those belongs to the guy working behind the counter in Yogurtland. I look up at the lamppost in front of the car illuminating the hood and shining through the windshield.

I open the door and slide into the driver's seat. Gazing into her eyes, for a moment I'm reminded of the last time my mom took me to get ice cream, when I was nine years old. I clench my jaw against the visceral nature of this memory and Senia takes this as an invitation.

She climbs into my lap and takes my face in her hands as she crushes her lips to mine. I thread my fingers into her hair and roughly grab a fistful of her dark locks. She whimpers as I thrust my tongue into her mouth and squeeze my fist around her hair, intermittently tightening my grip then easing up. Finally, I pull her head back by her hair and her eyes widen with shock and excitement. That's when I notice her styrofoam bowl of yogurt upended between us, the cold stickiness seeping through both of our shirts.

She smiles as she swipes her finger through the cool, sticky substance and slowly eases her finger into her mouth. 'Creamy,' she purrs.

'Fuck,' I whisper as my dick jumps, trying to escape my jeans.

I grab the bowl and toss it into the backseat and she smiles as I swipe my finger through the yogurt on her shirt then shove my hand under her skirt. Her thighs are smooth and warm against the back of my fingers as I move straight for her panties. She holds my gaze as I slip my fingers under the fabric and find her clit. She swallows hard, and her smile melts into an expression of pure ecstasy.

‘Oh my God,’ she breathes as I stroke her gently.

I grab the back of her neck and pull her mouth against mine, swallowing her moans as if they were the air keeping me alive. I shove two fingers inside her and she gasps as I curl my fingers to reach her spot. Her body folds into me as I lick the soft skin below her earlobe. I pull my hand from her panties. Her face is incredulous as I grab her shoulders and push her away.

‘Get in the back.’

For a moment, it seems as if she’s questioning this abrupt request. ‘This better be good,’ she says as she slithers between the two front seats to get into the backseat.

I reach under her skirt as she crawls into the back and yank down on her panties. ‘Jesus Christ, Tristan!’

‘Make up your mind,’ I say as I place my hand on her ass and push her into the backseat. ‘Am I Jesus Christ or Tristan?’

She laughs as I scramble into the backseat after her, holding on to her panties so she’s forced to leave them behind. I quickly position myself between her legs as she lies on her back and smiles. ‘You can be whoever the fuck you want.’

I slide my arm under her waist and lift her up so I can place her back against the passenger-side window. Pushing up her skirt, I spread her legs wide open and marvel at the sight of her. She’s perfectly shaved with a small landing strip of dark hair that ends at the top of her slit.

'I prefer Tristan,' I say, flashing her my crowd smile.

She whimpers like a kitten in pain, her hips writhing against me as I devour her slowly and methodically. She tastes like the frozen yogurt I smeared all over her.

'Oh, Tristan,' she moans and I hook my arms tightly around her thighs to steady her as her legs begins to tremble. 'Oh, my fucking God!'

I suck gently as her clit pulsates against my tongue. She lets out a loud cry that sounds like a sigh mixed with a scream. I can't help but smile as I continue to stimulate her until she grabs chunks of my shoulder-length hair and yanks me up.

'Holy shit,' she breathes as she wraps her arms around my neck and pulls me on top of her.

But she doesn't kiss me. She just holds me there and I quickly begin to feel uncomfortable with this closeness. I start to push away, but she tightens her grip.

'Please don't move,' she begs, and I can hear something strange in her voice – she's crying.

I lie still with her for a while until I no longer hear her sniffling. I slowly pull my head back to look her in the eye and she quickly wipes at the moisture on her cheeks.

'I'm sorry,' she whispers.

I grab her hand and pull it away from her face. 'It's okay,' I murmur, brushing my thumb over her cheekbone.

'No, it's not,' she says, a hard edge to her voice as her

hands reach down to undo the button and zipper on my jeans. 'But it will be.'

She pushes my boxers down until my dick springs free and I suck in a sharp breath as it comes in contact with her.

'I don't have a condom.'

My hair hangs around my face as I hover over her. She reaches up and pushes my hair back as she pulls my mouth to hers. I groan as I try to resist making such a stupid mistake. Despite the rumors, I don't have unprotected sex. I may be a whore like my mother, but I'm not as reckless as she is.

I try to pull my face back, but Senia holds my head still. Suddenly, I'm royally pissed off. I tear myself from her grasp and glare at her.

'This is just a fuck. Nothing more,' I insist and her eyebrows scrunch together. A sharp pang of regret twists inside my chest. 'I'm sorry.'

Why the fuck am I apologizing?

'Then shut up and fuck me,' she says, tightening her legs around my hips. The tip of my cock presses against her opening.

I slide in slowly, watching as she closes her eyes and tilts her head back. Leaning forward, I suck on her throat as I gradually ease myself further inside her with each stroke.

'You're tight as fuck,' I whisper as I carefully work my way deeper inside.

She doesn't respond, so I keep thrusting, slowly

at first then working my way up to a steady pace. I pull my head back to see her face and her eyes are still closed. I don't know why, but I want to see her eyes.

'Look at me,' I command, and she opens her eyes instantly, her gaze finding mine.

Her eyes are slightly red and that's when I notice the tear tracks running from the corners of her eyes, down her temple, and disappearing into her dark hair. A strange urge overcomes me and I lean down and kiss her temple. Licking my lips, the saltiness of her tears turns me on even more. I ease my hand behind her knee and lift her leg higher so I can thrust deeper.

She whimpers as she threads her fingers through my hair and pulls my mouth to hers. I kiss her slowly, matching the rhythm of my hips to the movement of our tongues. She bites my top lip and I feel myself getting so close to blowing my load.

'God damn,' I whisper as I try to pull my head back, but she holds my head still and kisses me deeply as I let go inside her.

My dick twitches as I fill her with my gushing warmth. I grunt into her mouth and she continues to kiss me, swallowing my cries the way I did hers. Finally, I tilt my head back and look her in the eye. Then I ask her a question I haven't asked anyone since I broke up with Ashley four years ago.

'Who was that on the phone?'

Chapter Two

Twelve Years Ago

I can hear her voice coming from the living room and I don't want to come out of my bedroom. She's so loud. I don't know why she always has to yell. She yells at me, at Grandma, and it won't be long before she starts yelling at Molly. Molly's only a baby. She doesn't know nothing about Elaine.

I don't call her Mom unless we're in the same room, and she's hardly ever here. Grandma takes care of Molly and me after school and whenever Elaine doesn't feel good – and that's a lot. *Why is Elaine already back here?* Tonight, we're spending the night at Grandma's so Elaine can be with her friends. I don't remember a lot of stuff that happened before we moved here to Raleigh a few months ago. But I do remember that I hate Elaine.

'Where's the fucking check? I know it came yesterday!' Elaine shouts at Grandma.

I can't stay in this bedroom. I have to protect Grandma. I slide off the bed and trudge across the grayish-blue carpet. Opening the bedroom slowly, Elaine's shouting gets louder.

'It hasn't come! And where are you going dressed like that?' Grandma shouts back, but her shouting doesn't sound like her daughter's shouting.

Grandma's voice is soothing and strong, but it's not harsh like Elaine's. I hate Elaine's voice.

I step into the living room and Elaine is wearing a dark-red dress that looks more like a sweater. It only covers her to the top of her legs and her black boots come up over her knee. She isn't dressed for the snow, which is probably why Grandma asked her why she's dressed like that.

'Where the fuck do you think I'm going, to get a fucking ice cream?' Elaine laughs and Grandma's round face scrunches up in disappointment.

Elaine's dark hair is messily flipped over to one side of her head. I didn't inherit her dark hair. Mine is light brown, probably like the sperm donor. That's what Grandma calls my father. I've never met him, but I think that's because Elaine doesn't know who he is. When I was seven, she told me that she wished she'd had an abortion. I didn't know what that was until I looked it up in the dictionary. That was two years ago. That was when I started calling her Elaine.

'You should take Tristan to get ice cream,' Grandma insists as Elaine digs through her big brown purse.

'It's fucking snowing,' Elaine replies with a chuckle. 'He can go outside and scoop some snow into a cup.'

The blonde girl standing next to Elaine lets out a low, rumbling laugh. I don't recognize this girl. Elaine's always bringing different girls to our house and Grandma hates it when she brings them here, ever since one of them threw up on her carpet. This girl looks younger than the other girls Elaine usually brings home, maybe sixteen or seventeen. Her eyes are covered in dark make-up and her mouth hangs open, making her look a little stupid.

The blonde looks at me and her top lip curls up. 'We should take him to get ice cream. I need some ice cream.'

Elaine glances at me then she goes back to digging through her purse. 'Fine. We'll get a fucking ice cream. At least it's too fucking cold outside for it to melt. Last thing I need is for him to make a mess all over Sadie's car.'

'I don't want ice cream,' I say as I scoot closer to Grandma.

That's when Molly starts to cry. She has a fever and Grandma has been fussing over her all night ever since Elaine brought us over here. Maybe I should pretend to have a fever.

Grandma pats me on the back. 'Go with your mom, Tristan. I have to take care of Molly.'

'I can help you,' I insist, but Grandma's already in the hallway on her way to her bedroom where she keeps Molly's playpen that Elaine hauls around everywhere.

Elaine rolls her eyes as she opens the front door for the blonde and me. 'Hurry up,' she says.

'I need to get a jacket.'

'You don't need a jacket. The ice cream parlor is indoors. Just get in the damn car.'

A whoosh of cold December air blasts me in the face as I step toward the front door. As I make my way out the door, my eyes repeatedly flit over to Grandma's purple sweater, which is draped over the arm of the sofa. I consider swiping it up and wrapping it over my shoulders, but purple is for girls. I'll look stupid and Elaine will make fun of me.

It's freezing inside the car. I could tell by the emblem on the hood that this is a Cadillac. The inside of the car smells like smoke and perfume and the gray leather in the backseat is cold as ice against the backs of my arms. I try to lean forward a little so it doesn't touch my skin, but I begin to get carsick from the way Elaine drives, so I just lean back and close my eyes.

A few minutes later, the car stops and I open my eyes when the engine stops rumbling. The blonde girl is looking over her shoulder at me from the front seat as Elaine touches up her make-up in the rearview mirror.

'What's his name again?' the blonde asks.

'Tristan. I named him after—' Elaine stops herself before she can finish this sentence. 'It doesn't matter. Let's go get a fucking ice cream so I can take him home. I have shit to do.'

The entire time we're standing in line, Elaine is

tapping her foot against the white tiled floor. When we make it to the front of the line, she doesn't even ask me what I want, she just orders a scoop of vanilla on a sugar cone. I hate vanilla.

I take my ice-cream cone from the man behind the counter and he can see the disappointment in my face. 'Is this not the flavor you want, kiddo?'

'Yes, it is,' Elaine replies quickly as she grabs my shoulders to turn me away from the counter. 'Come on, come on. Let's go sit down. I don't got all day.'

I take a few licks of the ice cream cone once we're seated in our plastic chairs at a small, round table. But then I think of a solution.

'I have to go to the bathroom,' I say as I stand from my chair.

'You can't go to the bathroom alone,' Elaine says as she pulls her cell phone out of her purse. 'Just hold it till you get home.'

The vanilla ice cream is starting to melt. I have to throw it away without her seeing. 'I can go by myself. I'm nine years old.'

'Charlene, take him to the bathroom,' she says as she begins dialing a number on her cell phone. 'I'll be outside.'

Charlene stands up, not bothering to bring her bowl of orange sherbet with her. 'Come on, kid.'

She grabs my shoulder to lead me forward and I wriggle out of her grasp. 'I can go to the bathroom by myself.'

The corner of her red lips curls up and my heart thumps against my chest as we near the bathroom. She reaches for the doorknob and opens the door for me. It's a private bathroom. No stalls, just a single toilet and a sink. It smells like cherry air freshener and it's almost as cold in here as it was in the Cadillac.

The lock clicks and she crosses her arms as she waits for me. 'We ain't got all day.'

The toilet is on the same wall as the door. If I take a piss, she'll see me from the side. All I wanted to do was throw away this damn ice cream, which is now dripping down my hand and wrist. She huffs as she takes the ice cream from my hand and tosses it into the garbage can next to the sink.

'What a mess. Come here so I can wash your hands.'

She pulls me toward the sink and turns on the water. It's cold so she turns on the hot water and waits until it warms up before she sticks my hands under the water. Her chest is pressed against my shoulders as she gently scrubs my hands with the slick soap. She begins massaging my fingers and I pull my hand away.

'Stop,' I mutter, trying to back away, but she's pressed against me, locking me in place.

'Your mom will kill me if you take your sticky fingers in the car. Just relax, Tristan.'

I swallow hard and try not to breathe too loudly as I let her rub my hands with the slippery soap. I close my eyes, trying not to let what I think is happening inside my pants actually happen. Not now. Please not now.

'Does that feel good?' she whispers and I shake my head fiercely. 'It's okay if it feels good.'

She wraps her fingers around my thumb and moves her fist slowly up and down. I want to scream for her to stop, but there are people sitting in tables outside the door. What will Elaine do if I make a scene? I'm not at home where Grandma will keep me safe.

'Do you have to use the potty?' the blonde asks as she reaches for the button on my jeans.

'No,' I say firmly as I push her hand away. I can't let her feel that thing growing in my pants. 'Stop. Please stop. I just want to go home. Please.'

'Tristan, your mommy said you have to do this or she won't take you home.' She reaches for my button again, but this time she waits until I finally move my hand away. 'That's a good boy. You'll like this. I promise.'

Chapter Three

'Get up.' The redhead in my bed – I think her name is Beth – rolls over and reaches for me. I slide out of bed and yank the comforter off in one swift motion. 'I said, *Get up*. You have to leave. I have plans.'

'What the fuck?' she squeals as she reaches for the sheet to cover up her naked body. I grab the sheet first and yank it off the bed. 'You're an asshole!'

I chuckle. 'Like you didn't already know that.'

She scrambles out of bed and quickly gets dressed. 'One of these days your dick is gonna fall off or somebody's gonna break your black heart. I'm just sorry I won't be there to see it.'

'Yeah, I'm really sorry for your loss.'

I follow her downstairs, smiling as she continues to lob insults at me. I open the front door for her to leave and she looks as if she's going to spit in my face. It wouldn't be the first time a girl has done that. But she doesn't spit; she just stares at me for a moment before she delivers her final blow. 'You were talking in your sleep,' she says with a grin.

I suppress the urge to stop her as she steps over the threshold and sets off down the gravel path to the roundabout where her Toyota is parked next to my Lightning. Despite the fact that she just pissed me off, I still stare at her ass until she's inside her car, but I don't bother watching her car drive away.

So she heard me talking in my sleep? Big fucking deal. I've heard that same line from other chicks a dozen times. Not a single one of those girls sold her story. Chris Knight's bassist isn't a juicy enough target for the tabloids, even though I've given them plenty of material over the years. And what's the worst thing she could have heard?

My stomach churns with the thought of the worst thing I could have said.

The shame morphs into anger and I punch the inside of the door. 'Fuck!' The pain shoots through my knuckles and the burn of broken skin is instantaneous.

I am not broken.

I close my eyes and repeat this mantra in my head a few times before I make my way into the kitchen. My cell phone buzzes on the granite countertop and I glance at the screen before I pick it up.

'What?'

'Xander said we have to be at Reverb in an hour.'

Chris's voice has an edge to it, like he's in pain but he's trying not to let it show. Typical Chris, putting Claire's and the band's needs before his own. Chris broke his leg a couple of months ago – a grotesque compound fracture – and since they cut off the cast a couple of weeks ago, the guy hasn't stopped running around like a crazy person. He's desperately trying to find a studio in the Triangle where we can record the new album. He even got the producer to agree to let us make this second album totally acoustic. All so he won't have to go to Los Angeles to record and leave Claire behind for the second time.

There are only two persons' needs that come before mine and I promised Molly and Grandma Flo I'd be there this morning. So I'll be there at the studio in an hour, but I'm going to see them first. If Chris and Jake have to wait a while then that's Chris's problem for calling me at the last minute.

'I'll be there,' I reply, then I end the call before Chris can ask me about my plans.

He knows I visit Molly and Grandma on Sundays, but he doesn't know that I'm visiting them today on a Monday. And I don't want him to know. Chris isn't the type to ask questions, but if he finds out why I'm visiting my grandmother today, he'll give me that look – the *I'm-not-going-to-say-anything-but-I'm-secretly-pitying-you* look. And I *really* don't want him to talk to Jake or Claire about this. I don't need anyone's sympathy.

I take a five-minute shower and speed over to my grandmother's house in Raleigh. It's thirty minutes from my house in Cary. As soon as I had enough money, I moved the fuck out of Raleigh. That city and that house are ripe with bitter memories. Plus, being out here means I don't have to get weekly visits from Elaine asking for money.

I paid to have Grandma's house renovated last January while we were on tour, so Molly wouldn't have to change schools. I wanted her to come live with me in Cary when I bought this place in August, but she didn't want to leave her friends behind. She's thirteen; she doesn't understand that leaving her friends behind in order to get away from Elaine is in her best interest. Unfortunately, this also means I haven't had Molly or Grandma over to see my house yet. I can't risk them giving Elaine my address. Like me, Elaine can be very convincing.

I pull up in front of the yellow two-bedroom house I grew up in and take a deep breath to prepare myself for this visit. Throwing open the car door, I'm not surprised when I hear the squeak of the front door opening and Molly's shoes slapping the pavement. As soon as I close my car door, she's rounding the front of my car.

'Gah! I missed you!' she squeals as she throws her arms around my waist.

I chuckle as I wrap my arms around her shoulders and squeeze her tightly. 'I missed you too, Moon.'

I gave Molly the nickname 'Moon' when she was three years old. She has a round, moon-like face that shines like moonbeams. And she used to beg me to read *Goodnight Moon* to her every night, until I turned twelve the next year and everything changed.

It wasn't until I met Chris in my seventh-grade math class that I realized I wasn't doomed to follow in my mother's footsteps. When he asked me if I wanted to start a band, he didn't know he was offering me a key out of my self-made prison.

As soon as I kiss her forehead, she starts to sob. 'Why are you crying?' I ask, though I already know.

Grandma Flo is sick. Since the day she took me away from Elaine when I was nine years old, she's been stronger than the rock this house was built on. But it turns out she's only human, after all. Three weeks ago, she was diagnosed with stage-four breast cancer after a routine mammogram showed a small lump the size of a grape. The tumor had nestled in at the base of her breast and attached itself to her chest wall where it began to spread to her left lung and lymph nodes around her neck and under her arm. Once the cancer reaches the lymph nodes, where the lymphatic fluid then carries the cancer cells to other places in the body, there's not much that can be done. The doctor labeled Grandma as T2 N2 M1 – Stage IV. A bunch of gibberish that basically means she's going to die.

'I don't want to be alone,' Molly whispers against my chest and I grit my teeth against all the anger that naturally follows moments like these.

'You're not going to be alone. People with stage-four cancer can live for several years.'

She lets go of me and walks toward the house without replying.

I only have ten minutes, so I bound toward the house and open the door for Molly. She walks in with her head down, unimpressed with this gesture. I follow her in and my stomach clenches at the sight of the living room. I had everything renovated to get rid of the memories, but you can't hide pain that runs this deep under a coat of beige paint.

Molly looks over her shoulder at me as she plods into the kitchen. 'She's in bed.'

I trudge through the hallway and slowly push open the door to Grandma Flo's room. She's asleep, curled up on her side with the blanket clutched tightly beneath her chin. Her short grayish-brown hair falls over her face as her chest rises and falls slowly. I kneel down next to her bed and reach for her.

Her eyebrows scrunch together as she tries not to cry. 'I'm sorry,' she whispers and her face forms an expression of unimaginable anguish.

I don't have to ask her why she's sorry. She's apologizing because she thinks she's not going to live long enough to take care of Molly until she's an adult. That's bullshit.

'Don't you apologize to me,' I reply, brushing her hair away from her soft cheek. 'You've got nothing to be sorry about.'

'I'm so tired. I couldn't sleep last night worrying about what's going to happen.'

'I'll go so you can get your rest. I have to be at the studio in a few minutes. I just wanted to check on you.'

In typical Grandma Flo style, she delivered the news of her diagnosis a couple of weeks ago as if she were merely remembering something she needed me to pick up from the grocery store. *Don't forget the eggs, and, by the way, I'm dying of cancer.* I could hear from the weariness in her voice that she wasn't feeling well when I called her yesterday to cancel my usual Sunday visit. But I had just finished taking five body shots of tequila off of Beth's creamy white naked skin. I was in no condition to rush over here to check on her last night.

I stand from Grandma's bed and hand her the box of tissues from her nightstand. 'Don't worry about Molly.'

'What about you?'

I think back to the last time I lived with Elaine nine years ago. I swore I'd never let anyone control me the way she did the summer before seventh grade. I also swore I'd never take my grandmother's love for granted.

'You know I'll be fine.'

She doesn't look convinced as she dabs a tissue at the corner of her blue eyes. Grandma Flo insists I need to settle down and let someone in. I almost did that with Ashley and I ended up getting my heart stomped on. No, not stomped on. Completely fucking extinguished. I'm not about to settle down any time soon. Besides, the only girls who want to settle down with me are the gold-diggers.

I kiss her forehead before I head out to my car. I turn the key in the ignition and lower the stereo as I try to compose myself. Maybe I *should* settle down if it would give my grandmother peace of mind in her final days. Settling down with a girl to please your dying grandmother sounds like something that would happen in some tragic love story that surely ends with death and at least one shattered heart. But I can't deny the appeal. I could pretend to be someone I'm not for a few months to make Grandma happy. Hell, I've been pretending to be someone I'm not for the past nine years. A few months will be a piece of cake.

It's settled. I'm going to get myself a girlfriend, maybe even a fiancée. This shouldn't be too difficult, especially since I already have a prime candidate in mind.

Chapter Four

I leave the recording studio with Senia's phone number, even though Chris refused to give it to me. He has a bad habit of leaving his phone unattended in the control room. It didn't take long to find Senia's phone number, and I swiped Claire's number as insurance, in case Senia tries to ignore my calls.

I'm not one to chase girls. But I'd be lying if I said that I haven't been thinking about Senia since our tryst outside the yogurt shop. When I asked her who she had been talking to on the phone, she pushed me off of her then quickly got dressed and left. I drove home licking the taste of her and the yogurt from my lips. I kept thinking back to all the times we'd almost had sex. Then I began to remember all the times I'd tried to have sex with her and she rejected me because she was in a relationship.

The worst memory I have of Senia has to be the time we almost had sex in the pub restroom in September. It was almost three months ago, but I still cringe when I think of the words I said to her. I actually said, 'You'll do,' as we were tearing at each other's clothes, as if I were settling for her. That's the kind of thing I'm used to doing: lashing out at someone who's rejected or hurt me in the past. I have to be prepared to approach things differently with Senia this time. I have to prepare myself for the inevitable rejection and I have to resist my desire to hurt her when it comes.

Pursuing Senia will also be complicated by her friendship with Claire and my friendship with Chris. It may also be the one shot I have at a normal, convincing relationship.

I climb into the driver's seat of my car and shoot her a text that works with most girls, even though I have a strong suspicion that Senia is not like most girls.

Me: *I was thinking about you while I was in the studio today.*

It's not a lie. I was thinking about her while I was hurriedly scrolling through the contacts on Chris's phone searching for her number. I tuck the phone into my pocket then peel out of the Reverb parking lot. By the time I pull into the driveway in front of my house in Cary, I'm certain that I'll have a response to my text.

I slide out of the driver's seat and slam the door before I activate the alarm. Slipping the phone out of my pocket, I see the notification that I have four text messages. I smile as I unlock my phone and navigate to the messaging app.

Molly: *Grandma said you don't have to come over tomorrow. Her insurance company is sending a van.*

Me: *Tell her to cancel the van. I'll be there at 11 like I said.*

I open the next message and I'm not surprised to see it's from Jenny.

Jenny: *My roommate is visiting family in Vermont. Want to come over?*

I met Jenny at the show we played in Durham last month. Her roommate hates me, which makes Jenny perfect. This means she has to keep me at a distance. Plus, she can do some pretty amazing things with her mouth. Normally, I'd jump on the chance for an easy fuck like Jenny, but something about waiting for Senia's text makes me hesitate.

Me: *Maybe some other time.*

The next text is from Chris, threatening to feed me to Rachel's Aunt Maddie if I text Senia. Rachel is Jake's girlfriend who became his fiancée last week. Not many people know that Rachel and Jake met in high school band class. Of course, Jake played the snare drum. Though Rachel grew up playing the piano, her mom made her attempt to take up the saxophone that year. Jake told me that he once caught her practicing a Kenny G song in her bedroom. Rachel threatened bodily harm if I ever tell anyone about this.

I take it, from Chris's text, he must have found the selfie I left on his phone today. The last text is from Rachel warning me that if I'm late to tomorrow's recording session she'll poison me slowly. Considering Chris rolled into the studio later than I did, he probably received an even more colorful version of this text. I don't know why the fuck Jake lets her be such a bitch to everyone. I would never allow my girl to bust my friends' balls like that.

The one time I called Jake out on this, it was Chris who answered for him. 'Rachel is only saying exactly what we're all thinking.' Chris may be like a brother to me and he may be the wisest asshole when it comes to charming the ladies, but he doesn't know shit about controlling them. Whether they admit it or not, women want to be dominated. They want to be owned.

Except for Senia, it seems, because she still hasn't responded to my text.

When I enter the house, Lily the cleaning lady is just gathering up her cleaning supplies and her vacuum cleaner to leave. I walk past her without acknowledging her presence and head straight for the kitchen. It smells like that lemon-scented cleaner she uses. I walk past the dining area and through the French doors onto the veranda.

I bought this house in September because I wanted to be far enough from Raleigh that I wouldn't have to worry about running into Elaine. Also, I wanted to be far enough that Grandma Flo and Molly wouldn't try to track me down and pay me any surprise visits. I've been living in this house more than two months and I can't decide what makes me feel worse: the fact that Molly and Grandma still don't know where I live or the fact that they haven't tried to figure it out.

I head past the outdoor dining table where I've made at least a half-dozen girls come until they were practically unconscious. Removing the metal grate from in front of the stone fireplace, I reach my hand inside and feel around over the rough stone. My hand hits the screw jutting out the inner surface of the chimney and my fingers follow the chain that hangs loosely from the screw. I pull the necklace off the screw and ball up my fist around it before I take a seat on one of the cushioned deckchairs.

My fist closes tightly around the gold chain with the heart pendant as I gaze out across the vast expanse of green grass behind the house that stretches out farther than my eyes can see. It's been four years since Ashley admitted to cheating on me and threw this necklace at my face. I don't know why I've kept it, other than to hold on to a reminder that relationships aren't worth the trouble. And the sickening suspicion in the pit of my gut that I'm just as worthless.

Leaning forward in the chair, I slowly open my fist. The gold is covered in soot, which coats the palm of my hand in dark striations that crisscross my skin. I stand up and chuck the necklace out onto the grass, so far that I'm certain it lands on my neighbor's property.

Good. It's someone else's trouble now.

Chapter Five

Three Days Later

'Elaine called this morning,' Grandma says as she drops the thawed turkey carcass into a bucket filled with ice and her special brine: a mixture of water, white wine, honey, salt, and various spices, which she drowns the turkey in the night before Thanksgiving. The tinny sound of Christmas music is playing from a clock radio on the counter as she leans over to pick up the bucket, which must weigh over forty pounds now with the turkey in it.

I reach down and take the bucket out of her hands. 'You shouldn't be cooking. You should be resting.' I don't bother acknowledging her comment about Elaine calling. She already knows how I feel about that. I don't want to know about anything to do with her.

'I'm not dead yet. I can't just lie there and feel sorry for myself. Put it on the counter.'

I heave the bucket onto the quartz countertop and watch as she begins pulling ingredients out of the fridge and the cupboards to make apple pie. She's wearing one of the many checkered blue and white aprons she makes by hand. Grandma Flo hasn't worked in twelve years, since Molly and I came to live with her. She used to live modestly off her savings and the life insurance money she received after Grandpa Ivan passed. Now *I* support her, though she refuses to buy or use more than she needs.

She grew up with very little in a different time when nothing was wasted and people helped their neighbors. It wasn't until she got married and Elaine was in school that she decided to get a job and be a bit more independent – less traditional. Grandma insists that the reason Elaine turned to drugs shortly after I was born was because she worked outside the home and Elaine spent a lot of time alone. It's a decision she has never stopped regretting. She never wanted Molly or me to feel like she was too busy for us. Now, all I can think of as I watch her sifting the salt into the flour is that she's been too busy for herself.

I pull a chair out from the kitchen table and move all the ingredients she just placed on the counter onto the table. She shakes her head as I hold the chair out for her, but she reluctantly takes a seat. I grab the bowl of apples and she smiles as I begin peeling them for her.

'Don't forget to squeeze some lemon juice on the apples so they don't brown,' she warns me.

'I can't believe I'm making a damn apple pie.'

'You should put on an apron. I'm sure you'll catch some girls if you post a photograph of that on the Facebook.'

I grab a lemon out of the fruit bowl on the counter and cut it in half to squeeze some juice over the peeled apples. 'You'd better not tell anyone I did this,' I say as I kiss the top of her head. 'I'll be back in a few hours. Do you need me to bring anything back?'

'Bring me some brown sugar and one of those bottles of sparkling cider Molly likes.'

'Will do.'

I hurry out to my car, eager to get out of the house before Molly gets back with her friend Carissa. Thirteen-year-old girls with crushes are not as cute as they seem. Most thirteen-year-old girls these days have been exposed to enough internet porn to think they know what they're doing. Carissa's crush on me only seems to grow stronger the more I avoid her, but the alternative is making friends with her and that's just plain disgusting.

I pull out of the driveway and head to the local pub where Chris and I used to chill out every Wednesday night, before he decided to go solo last year. Everything's changed since then. We're only twenty-one, but look at us. Chris has a kid he's fighting to know. Jake is getting married. We're fucking adults. And what am I doing? I bought a fucking house.

I enter the bar and immediately take the second-to-last stool from the end of the bar. Chris used to sit in the last seat and old habits are hard to break. Link, the bartender, nods as he finishes pouring a beer for a guy with a long gray beard. I don't recognize the guy, but I haven't been here in over a year. He could be a new regular.

Link slides the beer in front of the guy then heads over to me. 'What's up, bro? Long time no see.'

Link has more tats and piercings than Chris and me combined, which is saying a lot considering Chris is fucking addicted to ink. I only have nine tats. I've been holding off on getting the tenth one because I've convinced myself that it's going to be some fucking special occasion.

'Get me a Pliny,' I say as we shake hands. 'I'm so fucking over this holiday shit.'

'You need some pussy,' Link says as he reaches into the fridge under the bar and pulls out a cold Pliny the Elder. 'You remember my girl Tara? Her friend Chrissy is coming in to pick up something in just a few minutes. You should hit that.'

As easy as that, he's just pimping out his girlfriend's best friend, like he's so sure she's just going to do whatever the fuck I want. Well, she probably will, but the point is that I'm not the only one who does this. I'm not the only one who thinks of a woman as a means to an end. Fuck Chrissy and feel better about myself, maybe relieve some stress. Is it normal to think of another human being as a tool to be used as a fucking form of therapy? I don't know. But after five beers and two shots of whiskey, when Chrissy walks in with her pink scarf wrapped around her neck and her tight jeans hugging a luscious ass, I don't fucking care.

I stare at the way her breasts rest on the bar when she leans over it as Link reaches into a cup next to the cash register and pulls out a set of keys. He hands her the keys and she squints at me as she turns to leave.

'Make sure you keep the fire going until we get there tomorrow morning,' Link says to her. 'That cabin is cold as fuck right now.'

She nods without looking at him, her eyes glued to me. 'You're Chris Knight's—'

'Bassist,' I say, trying not to let her see how annoying it is that hardly anyone knows me as anything other than Chris's bassist. 'And you're Chrissy. I've heard *all* about you. You need some help getting the fire started in that cabin?'

She smiles shyly and for a moment I think she's going to turn down my offer, then she nods.

I plunk down a hundred-dollar bill and my car keys on the bar. 'Bring my car tomorrow?' I ask Link and he nods, then I slip my hand under her scarf and her blonde hair to grab the back of her neck as I lead her outside. I do this partially because I'm unsteady on my feet from the alcohol and partially because girls love when you grab them by the neck. It all goes back to that ownership thing. It's fucking ridiculous how predictable women are.

A dull pang of guilt registers in my belly. I should be

driving to the grocery store to get Grandma's Thanksgiving goods, but I can't drive drunk. Might as well burn off this alcohol with my favorite kind of cardio. I'll be back at Grandma's tomorrow morning in time to help with whatever she needs for T-Day dinner.

When we reach the parking lot, I'm a little put off by her white Lexus. Either this girl has money or she's driving someone else's car. As if she can read my thoughts, she blurts out, 'This is my mom's car.' She hits the key fob to disable the alarm and I seize this small moment of distraction to grab her face and kiss her hard. She whimpers as I push her against the car and press my body against hers.

She tastes like black licorice and it almost triggers my gag reflex. I hate licorice. I pull my face back and stare at her for a second as she attempts to catch her breath.

I feel nothing.

Everything is exactly as it should be.

'Let's go,' I whisper and she hastily sets off to the driver's side.

I slide into the beige leather passenger seat then lean my head back and close my eyes as I try not to reach into my pocket for my phone. No drunk texting tonight. Tonight, I'm going to fuck Chrissy into a stupor. I'll worry about the rest tomorrow.

Chapter Six

I wake up just after 7 a.m. with Chrissy's cheek resting on my abdomen just above my dick. She's laying crosswise on the bed and my hand is on her back. Her ass is even nicer with her clothes off. My head is killing me and I have a vague memory of Chrissy telling me that Link, his girlfriend, and Link's family would be here in the morning to celebrate Thanksgiving. It's 7 a.m. We still have time for one more goodbye fuck.

I slide my hand over her ribs and reach over to grab her breast. She groans softly as she turns over to face me, her head still resting on my abdomen. Her makeup is smeared all over her eyes and her lips look a little swollen, but definitely still fuckable.

'Sit up,' I order her and she looks confused.

'What time is it?'

'Seven o'clock. Sit up.'

Her eyes widen as she sits up on her knees. 'They're gonna be here in less than an hour!' she cries. 'We have to clean up.'

Her eyes dart around the dimly lit bedroom in the cabin, which isn't really a cabin. It's a tiny house on a farm forty-five minutes outside of Raleigh. Though it does look like a cabin from the outside, there isn't a mountain in sight.

'Calm down. An hour is plenty of time.'

I sit up and grab the back of her neck. She looks me in the eye as my other hand slides between her legs. Her panic melts as I stroke her clit. I tangle my fingers in her hair and pull her up until we're both standing on our knees on the mattress facing each other. She whimpers as I plunge two fingers inside her wet pussy to unearth her moisture. I hook my middle finger inside her, using my thumb to keep pressure on her clit as I massage her G-spot. Her shoulders begin to curl inward as she gets close to climax, but I tighten my grip on her hair and pull her head up.

'Do you want me to finish you?'

'Yes!' she cries, panting between gasps. 'Yes, please.' I ease the pressure off her clit and her mouth drops open as I remove my finger from inside her. 'No, no, please. Please finish,' she begs as she reaches for my hand.

I grab her hand and force it behind her back as I lean in and whisper in her ear. 'I'll finish you, but first you have to sit back and do what I say.'

She nods her head and immediately obeys when I instruct her to lie back with her shoulders against the headboard. I'm out of condoms so I'll have to make do with what's available. I straddle her chest and her eyes widen at the sight of my cock in front of her face.

'That's . . . that's kind of big,' she whispers.

'Don't worry. I'll go easy on you.'

I slide my hand behind her head, to control the movement and to protect her head from the headboard, then I slide into her mouth. I go slow at first, to let her adjust to my girth, but she soon reaches around to grab hold of my ass and push me farther inside. The pressure of her lips and the warm wetness of her tongue are perfect, but her teeth are killing me.

'Open your mouth wider,' I groan and she mutters something I can't understand with my cock in her mouth. 'Fuck.' I can't fuck her. I'm out of condoms and I'm not making that mistake again, but I can't take the scraping. I pull out of her mouth and her lips look red and stretched. 'Turn around.'

She quickly turns onto her belly and I grab her waist to pull her hips up into the air. I shake my head to shake off the doubts then I glide an inch into her pussy, just to get my dick wet, then I pull out. She gasps as I slide my heat between her cheeks and press gently against the opening.

'Feel free to scream,' I say as I slide inside, just a smidge farther with each stroke.

She buries her face in the pillow with the flannel pillowcase to muffle her screams and I'm glad for that when I hear my phone vibrating on the nightstand. I should let it ring, but my thoughts bounce to all different sorts of scenarios. Maybe Grandma's calling about the brown sugar I was supposed to bring her last night, or Molly is calling for her cider. Or maybe it's Senia finally coming to her senses.

I quickly pull out of Chrissy and reach for the phone. When I glimpse the name on the screen, I can't believe my eyes. It's Elaine. She knows I'll never answer her calls, so I'm not sure why she even tries. I hit the ignore button and I'm not at all surprised when I look down and see I've lost my erection.

I look back at my phone and see a voicemail notification from Molly. I press the play icon and listen: '*Tristan – wait! Oh, sh—*'

I laugh as I imagine her dropping her phone. I'll call her back once I'm out of here.

'Who the fuck was that?'

'You have a dirty mouth,' I tell Chrissy as I hurry up and start gathering my clothes off the wooden floor to get dressed.

'Are you leaving?' she shrieks as I pull on my pants.

'You said your friends are getting here at eight. It's seven thirty.' I pull on my shirt and shoot off another text to Senia wishing her a Happy Thanksgiving. She can't ignore me forever.

'Don't you at least want my number?' she says as she jumps out of bed and follows me to the front door naked.

'No.'

'Fuck you!'

'Already fucked you and it wasn't that great.'

She swings her open hand at my face, but I open the door in time to block it. Her hand smacks the inside of the door hard enough that it makes me a little nervous.

'Your hand okay?' I say with a chuckle, but I quickly slam the door shut as she reaches back to take another shot.

I laugh as I turn around and Link and his girlfriend, whose name I can't remember, are coming up the paved stone walkway.

'You bastard,' Link says with a smile as he slaps my keys into the palm of my hand. 'I knew you'd hit that.'

'You guys are pigs!' his girlfriend shouts, elbowing Link in the stomach as she makes her way to the front door.

'Do you always have to resort to violence?' he barks at her.

'You might want to give her a few seconds to get dressed,' I say over my shoulder.

Link shakes his head, a smirk materializing beneath his painful grimace. 'Happy Thanksgiving, bro.'

'Same to you.'

I slide into the driver's seat and immediately attempt to call Molly. After four rings, I get her voicemail greeting.

Why are both Molly and Elaine trying to reach me?

I hang up and toss the phone onto the passenger seat as I pull away from the cabin and start off down the long dirt road that leads off the farm and onto the highway. I speed along the highway back to Raleigh, shaving a good ten minutes off the forty-five-minute drive.

When I pull up next to the curb outside Grandma Flo's, I'm not surprised to see Elaine's shitty Nissan parked in the driveway. If it weren't Thanksgiving and if I weren't so worried, I'd peel the fuck out of here. I rush out of the car, not at all looking forward to seeing Elaine when I'm hungover and wearing last night's clothes. But I guess it's better that she thinks I'm a worthless drunk who's pissing his millions into the toilet. The less she knows about me the better.

I race up the front steps then open the door, preparing my psyche for the inevitable rage that will follow the sight of her emaciated face. The living room is empty, so I quickly move to the only logical place for Grandma to be on Thanksgiving morning: the kitchen. The kitchen is also empty and the turkey is still swimming in the bucket of brine. Grandma usually gets it into the oven by 6 a.m. Something's wrong.

Chapter Seven

Senia

The gods of Thanksgiving and I have a secret pact: I eat all their tasty offerings and they agree to not let me vomit or gain more than five pounds. Unfortunately, they never seem to hold up their end of the bargain on the weight gain and, when December rolls around, I find myself renewing my pact with the treadmill gods. But I think I may have been a bit overenthusiastic in my commitment to consuming the tasty offerings of the day. I feel sick, which gives me the perfect opportunity to skip out on family karaoke hour so I can handle some *covert* business.

Once Claire is deeply entrenched in a karaoke battle with my cousin Nico, I sneak out of the family room and race upstairs. It's a few minutes past one in the afternoon. Tristan texted me about six hours ago. I know I'm going to regret this.

Me: *Thanks for the kind message. Now kindly stop texting me. I'm not interested in being one of your concubines.*

I actually get a pain in my chest after I hit send. I know I'm supposed to hate Tristan and I'm sure as hell not supposed to talk to him, but I can't help but feel like I'm misjudging him. Like we're all misjudging him.

That's so stupid! That's exactly what guys like him want girls to think. Oh, poor misjudged Tristan who fucks anything that breathes.

I met Tristan a little more than three years ago after a show they played in Durham. Claire and I had been friends for a total of five weeks, but I already knew, from the moment she shared her love of *Vampire Diaries* with me, that she and I were destined to be best friends forever. She actually had to drag me to the show. I was pretty shy before college. Most of my friends throughout junior high and high school were math geeks, like me. Unfortunately, none of my high school friends ended up attending UNC Chapel Hill. Starting from scratch is difficult for any eighteen-year-old, but for a kid with moderate social anxiety, it's torture. Thankfully, Claire supported me through my *drink-till-you-don't-give-a-fuck* stage of development. So, of course, the first thing I did when I arrived at the club in Durham to watch Chris, Tristan, and Jake perform was get shit-faced drunk.

Needless to say, my eyes were glued to Tristan all

night as crazy thoughts of marriage and babies – and hot sex – raced through my socially inept and highly inebriated brain. Eventually, about halfway through the show, he finally cast his smoky gaze in my direction and smiled – a smile that I would later learn he and Chris refer to as their *crowd smile*. But, let me tell you, when he directed that smile my way . . . I'm not ashamed to say that I think I may have peed a little.

I am definitely *never* going to text him again. Unless it's to send him a pic of my awesome bunion, as I promised Claire.

Never. Again.

Tristan: *Whatever you say.*

Great! Now *I* feel like an asshole.

No. I will not allow him to do this to me. I will not text him again.

I sigh as I lie back on my bed and close my eyes. I try to push the images from that day outside Yogurtland out of my head, but it's no use. It's all I've been able to think about for the past twelve days. It was so different from all the other times Tristan and I have come close to having sex. It was almost as if seeing me on the phone with someone else spurred some competitive streak inside of him and he needed to outdo Eddie. And, let's be honest, as amazing as Eddie is in bed, he could never be Tristan.

What the hell am I thinking? Stop it, Senia!

Oh, great. Now I'm yelling at myself inside my head.

It wasn't just the sex. He wanted to know who I was talking to on the phone. That's not just sex, right?

No, it was sex combined with typical male territorial issues. It wasn't just sex. It was a fucking pissing contest. I am not anyone's property! Especially not anyone's property to piss on.

Okay, that settles it. I am not texting him back.

Me: *Are you okay?*
Tristan: *No. I'm at the hospital.*
Me: *What's wrong?*
Tristan: *Can I call you later?*

Shit! I'm so stupid. I stare at the text for a few minutes before I begin typing. The bedroom door flies open and Claire walks in. I quickly tuck the phone underneath me before I can finish typing my response.

'What are you doing in here?' she asks, looking winded and flushed from singing.

'Nothing. Just trying to digest the twenty pounds of food I've eaten. No better way to make sure it goes straight to my ass than lying down and doing *absolutely nothing*.'

Claire raises an eyebrow. 'Why are you acting like I just caught you masturbating?'

I laugh as I sit up and discreetly push my phone underneath my pillow. 'Please. You've caught me masturbating plenty of times.'

'Oh God, please. I don't want to talk about you touching yourself.'

'Whatever. Let's go downstairs. I think I'm ready for some more pumpkin pie.'

I glance over my shoulder at the pillow and shake my head as I close my bedroom door.

Chapter Eight

The emergency-room doors open and I race through, clutching the note Molly left on the refrigerator: *Went with Grandma to hospital. She wasn't breathing. Get here quick. Don't call me. I dropped my phone in the toilet.*

The entrance to the emergency waiting room is right before me. I storm in and find Molly sitting in a chair in the far corner with Elaine two chairs away from her. Molly's eyes are closed as she leans her head back against the wall. Her light-brown hair is pulled up into a messy bun at the top of her head – the way she always does it before she goes to bed. Elaine looks at me and I quickly look away as I head for Molly. I shake her knee and she jumps a little as she opens her eyes.

'Shit!' she cries as she's startled awake.

I've told Molly that she needs to stop cursing so much, but that's like trying to tell a fish to stop breathing water. She grew up with me as her role model. She's always looked up to me and, unfortunately, I haven't always set the best example.

'What happened?' I ask her as she sits up straight in the mauve chair.

'She took too many of those pain pills the doctor gave her,' Molly replies.

From the corner of my eye, I can see Elaine leaning forward as if she's going to get in on this conversation. She knows I won't speak to her. I haven't spoken to her in nine years. I don't care if she thinks her presence here earns her Brownie points. There's no good deed she can do that will ever make me think she is anything other than a selfish, depraved human being.

'Is she okay?' I ask, still unsure whether I want to take a seat next to Molly.

'Yeah. They know she wasn't trying to commit suicide because they have her medical records, so we don't have to wait for the psychiatrist to check her out. They're just keeping her here for another few hours until her blood pressure comes back up, then we can take her home.'

'She needs someone to keep an eye on her.'

Elaine's voice makes my skin prickle. Molly glances at her then back to me, foolishly wondering if I'm going to respond.

'I'm going to the cafeteria. You want to come with me?' I ask Molly and she nods as she stands from the chair.

After a long silence, punctuated by the occasional squeak of our sneakers against the shiny floor in the hospital corridors, Molly finally says something. And what she says makes me sick.

'I think you should talk to her.'

She doesn't have to say her name for me to know she's talking about Elaine. I pretend not to hear her, but she doesn't give up.

'I'm serious. Do you want Grandma to die thinking that you never spoke to her again?'

'Don't use Grandma in your emotional blackmail scheme.'

'You're so selfish.'

I get a flash of pain in my chest at these words spoken from Molly's lips. 'Don't say that.'

'I'm sorry,' she says as we turn into the cafeteria. Her face scrunches up as if she's trying to keep from crying. 'I'm just so scared of having to live with her.'

'That will never happen. Go sit down. I'll get you something.'

She rolls her eyes as she heads for a table in the corner. I make my way through the cafeteria line behind two other bleary-eyed patrons. I grab a couple of turkey sandwiches from the refrigerator case and some juice. When I arrive at the table with my tray of food, Molly's elbows are propped on the table and her face is buried in her hands.

'Eat your turkey dinner,' I order her, but she doesn't move. Then I see the glistening puddle of tears on the surface of the table.

'She's gonna die,' she whispers. 'Why?'

'Because life fucking sucks.'

'Not the answer I wanted.'

'It's the truth.' I unwrap the plastic wrap on her turkey sandwich and push the tray toward her. 'You can't expect anything good to last or you'll always be disappointed. Everything dies.'

She groans as she wipes the tears from her eyes and looks up. 'Why do you have to say stuff like that?'

'You need to be prepared.'

'You need to talk to Elaine and tell her I'm going to live with you. She was blabbing to me in the waiting room about how nice her new apartment in Durham is.'

'Nice compared to what? A fucking cardboard box?'

'I don't want to live with her. She said she has a new boyfriend.'

'You're not going to live with her.'

I lean back in the uncomfortable steel chair and try not to think of what I'll have to do to prevent Molly from being placed with Elaine. No one knows what Elaine is capable of except for me. Everyone thinks she's just a drug addict with a long list of ex-boyfriends and STDs. If I have to tell everyone the kind of person she really is, I will do it – for Molly's sake. I've never told anyone, not even Chris, about the summer before seventh grade.

My phone vibrates in my pocket and I pull it out

immediately. When I see the name on the screen, it's as if the clouds have parted and shined a light on this tiny corner of the hospital cafeteria. Then I read the message and I resist the urge to throw my phone across the room.

Senia: *Thanks for the kind message. Now kindly stop texting me. I'm not interested in being one of your concubines.*

I probably don't deserve anything better than this from Senia, but it still feels like a kick in the nuts right now. In any case, I don't have it in me to chase her any more. It was sort of fun for the last twelve days to bug her with cheesy text messages, but it just feels stupid and pathetic now.

Me: *Whatever you say.*

Molly stands up and I grab her hand before she can leave. 'Where are you going?'

'I have to go to the restroom. Want to join me?'

'You think that's funny, but I actually—'

'Potty-trained me. I know. You've told me a million times. It's gross.'

'Get out of here before I tell everyone in this cafeteria about the time you shit in Grandma's flower pot.'

'There's no one here.'

'Then I'll write a song about it.'

'You haven't written anything in years,' she mutters, then she walks away.

My phone vibrates again and a tremor of regret reverberates inside me for all the ways I haven't been good enough for Molly. I must be such a fucking disappointment to her. I used to write songs for her all the time and I'd sing her to sleep. I stopped writing three years ago. It's pointless. No one needs me to write songs. They need me to play my fucking instrument and bring the band the occasional bit of bad press.

I turn my phone over on the table to check the screen and this message brings the faintest hint of a smile to my lips.

Senia: *Are you okay?*
Me: *No. I'm at the hospital.*
Senia: *What's wrong?*

I don't have to tell her anything. Something tells me that Senia will probably come running to my side if I speak the right empty promises. But I really don't feel like fucking her.

I just need to talk.

Me: *Can I call you later?*

She makes me wait a torturous forty minutes for her response. Molly is back from the restroom and seated across from me, using my phone to text her friends, but even Molly smiles when she sees the text message pop up on my screen.

Senia: *Fine. But you'd better not tell me you're pregnant.*

Chapter Nine

Once the doctor releases Grandma, I help her to my car and Molly climbs into the backseat. Grandma's blood pressure was still on the low side, so they asked us to keep a close eye on her and to make sure she gets plenty of rest.

'Molly will make the turkey tomorrow,' I assure her as she leans her head back and closes her eyes.

'The turkey's been sitting there in that brine for too long. It's no good any more,' she replies softly. 'I'm sorry I screwed up. I just didn't know what else to do. I couldn't fall asleep.'

'Grandma, why don't you just try the chemo?'

'Because it won't do a damn thing but make me sicker. I don't want you two cleaning up my messes. I just want to go quietly.'

Molly sniffles loudly in the backseat and I resist the urge to look in the rearview mirror. I don't want to see what this is doing to her.

'I'm sorry, sweetheart,' Grandma says, reaching into

the backseat to comfort Molly. 'I don't mean to scare you.'

'Too late,' Molly grumbles. 'Can you take me to Carissa's?'

'No, you're staying home with me and Grandma.'

She groans roughly, the sound garbled by the tears clogging her throat.

'Just take her to her friend's house,' Grandma insists.

I crane my neck a little to get a look at Molly in the rearview mirror and I find her hugging her knees, tears streaming down her cheeks. Normally, I'd tell her to get her dirty shoes off my leather seats, but she doesn't need that; she needs a friend.

After I drop her off at Carissa's, Grandma and I arrive home a few minutes later and I'm overcome with a pang of guilt as I remember that I never brought Grandma the brown sugar or cider she asked for. I help her out of the car, though she keeps insisting I stop all this fussing over her.

By the time she's taken a bath and slid under her covers, I've cleaned up all the half-prepared food in the kitchen and refrigerator – to purge the house of all reminders. Then I sit back on the sofa and sigh. This is it. The moment I've been looking forward to and dreading all day.

I haven't had a conversation with a girl, on the phone, for . . . years. I'm not sure what possessed me to ask Senia if I could call her. All I know is that I want to hear her voice. Just the thought of needing anything – anyone – like this is terrifying.

'You are going to hate me,' she says.

This is not the greeting I expected when I dialed her number, but I'm intrigued. 'Why am I going to hate you?'

I half expect her to tell me that she doesn't have time to talk or that, on second thought, she really *does* want me to stop texting her. But the two words she whispers next make my balls shoot straight into my throat.

'I'm pregnant.'

'What the fuck? Is this a joke?'

'I wish.'

These two words catch me even more off guard, then it hits me. 'Wait a minute. If you're pregnant, why did you tell me to stop texting you?'

'I'm sorry. I didn't know when I sent you that text message. But then I got sick a couple of hours later, and I knew something was wrong. Thanksgiving is *my* holiday! I can eat an entire pumpkin pie and not get sick. I was made for this day. Then I realized I'm two days late. I'm so lucky Claire's gone for the night. She can't know anything about this.'

'Whoa, whoa. Slow down. Do you keep pregnancy tests on hand for this sort of thing?'

She clears her throat nervously. 'Um, yes. You don't want to know what I have in my goodie drawer.'

I chuckle. 'Actually, I think I *do* want to know. I want to know very badly.'

'Shut up. This is serious shit. I'm pregnant!' She whisper-shouts the last two words and this makes me smile.

I've never gotten anyone pregnant. Before I found out about Grandma a few weeks ago, I was always extremely careful not to become reckless like Elaine. I suppose I should be disappointed in myself, but I can't help feeling a sense of pride for my little swimmers. They did their job on the very first try, as if they'd been training for this performance all their lives. Well, I guess they have had lots of practice.

'So what do you want to do?' I ask. I think that's what I'm supposed to ask. I don't think telling her to get an abortion is the way these things are handled, but I doubt either one of us is ready for a baby.

Then an evil but brilliant idea flashes in my mind. I immediately try to push it out, but it keeps nagging and poking me as I wait for Senia's response.

'I don't know.'

Crap. She's crying.

'I'm not trying to tell you to get rid of it,' I insist.

She chuckles. 'Yeah, like *you* want to have a kid. You'd probably rather get cancer.'

I can't even move my lips to form a response to cover up what I'm feeling right now. She had no way of knowing what she just said would affect me so deeply, but she can sense something in my silence.

'I'm sorry. That was a real jerk thing to say considering I have no idea why you were at the hospital today.'

'It's okay. You didn't know. My grandma . . . She has stage-four breast cancer.'

'Oh, no. And I was telling you to stop texting me and now I'm calling you to tell you I'm pregnant. Oh God. I feel so selfish. I'm so sorry.'

She starts crying again and I get a strange urge to kiss her tears, to taste them the way I did before.

'You don't have to be sorry. You didn't know. But I have a way you can make it up to me.' She groans and I laugh. 'Not sexual favors. I was kind of hoping you might want to come hang out for a little while. My sister's gone so I have to stay here to keep an eye on my grandma. It's kind of lonely.'

Did I really just say, *It's kind of lonely*? What the fuck is wrong with me?

'Did you just tell me you're lonely?'

'You know you want to come over,' I say, trying to recover a bit of my dignity.

She sighs before she responds and the sound of her breath in my ear gives me goosebumps. 'Text me the address.'

Chapter Ten

I hear her car pull up outside – not that I'm listening for it. I immediately click off the TV show I'm watching about man caves and leap off the sofa. When I open the front door, Senia's walking up the path in a sapphire-blue dress that hugs her curves, a black trench coat and black heels.

'Did you get dressed up to come here?' I ask with a grin and she rolls her eyes.

'Well, I wasn't lying in bed in a fucking trench coat and heels, but I was wearing this dress. I always wear dresses. You know that.'

I do know that, yet, even with the easy access of simply pulling up her dress, this didn't make it easy enough for us to hook up until last week; until she was wearing a skirt. Maybe the dresses are a curse. I should rip it off her right now to find out.

Settle down, Tristan.

When she steps inside the house, I find myself feeling a bit self-conscious. The house looks fine.

It's pretty tiny, but it's completely remodeled. I can't remember if Senia has ever been here, but I don't want to admit this.

'It looks different,' she says as she looks around. 'I guess you and Chris really took care of your families after you hit the big time. What's that like?'

'What's *what* like?'

She turns to me and fixes me with a worried stare. 'Having a family to take care of?'

Her words stop me cold. 'I never really thought of it that way. I just do it because it's my job and . . . and I love them.'

She shakes her head as she looks away. 'I've never had to take care of anyone. Even when Sophie was a baby, my parents never made me change diapers or babysit. My older sisters did that. I don't know how to act like a mother, much less be one.'

'You want to take off that coat?' I ask as I shut the front door.

'I'm fine. I can't stay too long. I just wanted to talk about . . . you know.'

'Sit down,' I say, placing my hand on her back to guide her toward the sofa. As soon as I feel the coolness of her coat under my hand, a worried thought crosses my mind. 'Is this coat warm enough for the snow? Snow season starts in a few weeks. Do you need another coat?'

She takes a seat on the sofa and looks up at me as if I'm an alien. 'I have other coats, thanks.'

I sit next to her and chuckle as she scoots a few inches away from me. 'Are you afraid of being close to me?'

'Yes.'

'I can keep my hands to myself. You sure you don't want to take that off?' I ask, giving her sleeve a soft tug.

'I thought you said you could keep your hands to yourself.'

'I didn't touch you. I touched your coat.'

She narrows her eyes at me and leans back to get more comfortable. 'Aren't you going to offer me something to drink?'

'You can't drink in your condition.'

'Why, yes, I'd love a glass of water. Thank you.'

I smile as I make my way into the kitchen and take a glass out of the cupboard above the sink. I head for the refrigerator to get some water from the door, but the sound of the house phone stops me. I hurry back to the living room to grab the phone off the receiver. I don't want the ringing to wake up Grandma.

'Hello?'

'Hello. This is Carissa's mother. I'd like to speak to Molly's mother or father. Are they home?'

'This is her brother. What happened to Molly?'

'I really think I should speak to her parents.'

'They're not here,' I snarl. 'Where's Molly?'

'Well, that figures. Molly is in Carissa's bedroom . . . drunk. Somebody needs to come pick her up.'

'I'll be there. What's the address?'

Carissa's mother hangs up after she gives me the address and I stare at the phone for a moment, in shock.

'What's wrong?' Senia says, reaching for the empty glass I set down on the coffee table in front of her.

'My sister Molly's drunk. I have to go pick her up.'

'Drunk? Isn't she, like, ten?'

'She's thirteen.' I toss the phone onto the sofa and she quickly stands up.

'I'll go get her. You have to stay here with your grandma.'

I look at her and I'm surprised to see that she's serious. She wants to pick up my drunk, teenage sister. *Fuck. Molly's drunk.* Well, what did I expect? She's seen me drink away my troubles for about nine years. And I don't think my troubles will ever compare to the pain she must be feeling over Grandma.

'You don't have to do that,' I reply. 'I doubt this is how you wanted to spend your Thanksgiving.'

'Hey, I have a lot to be thankful for today. Let me do this . . . as a friend.'

I can't help but smile at these last three words. 'I think we're way past that,' I say, reaching into my pocket for my car key. I grab her hand and she swallows hard as I softly place the key in her palm. 'Take my car.'

Chapter Eleven

Senia

Tristan programs the address into the GPS in his silver sports car then stands back and watches as I put on my seatbelt. I'm having a little trouble getting the buckle into the slot with my shaky hands. I can't believe he's entrusting me with this thing, but he insists that if Molly is going to throw up in the car, he'd rather she do it in his than mine.

'Remember, this is a British car, so the GPS has a British accent,' he says with a warm smile. 'And don't press too hard on the brakes or the accelerator. Just let yourself get a feel for the car. This ain't a Ford Focus.'

'Ha, ha. I don't have the Focus any more. I gave it to Claire, remember?'

Oh, what would Claire think of me now? Driving Tristan's car . . . picking up his drunk sister . . . carrying his *child!*

'Yeah, that was very generous.' His eyes get a little unfocused as his mind wanders off, then he blinks a few times and looks me in the eye. 'Be nice to her when you pick her up. She's losing the most important person in her life.'

I nod and turn away from him, pretending to look at the passenger seat as he closes the door. I crank the key in the ignition and attempt to keep from crying as I recall my Grandma Elena. She passed when I was ten, but she had lived with us all my life. My mom wouldn't let me go to the funeral. She said I wasn't old enough. One day she was there, sitting on the sofa watching Mexican soap operas. The next day she was gone. That was eleven years ago and I still expect to see her sitting there every time I come home.

I can't imagine what Molly must be feeling right now, but I do know that she probably needs something that no one can give her: a promise that everything will be okay.

I have a very choppy drive to Carissa's house on Bedford Avenue near Pollock Place Park. I get a weird feeling in the pit of my stomach when I see the name Pollock Place Park. It makes me think of Tristan Pollock, then I think of Yesenia Pollock. *So stupid.* Tristan is not the marrying kind, even if he is acting like a complete weirdo since our meeting at Yogurtland.

I pull up in front of a house on the corner of Bedford and Taylor and take a deep breath as I shut off the engine. A woman with brown, frizzy hair is standing in the threshold of the front door with her arms crossed and a sour expression that matches her shitty sweater. This woman does not want to mess with me when I'm hormonal.

I climb out of the car and stuff the car key into my coat pocket. She looks surprised to see me. Then she steps aside and Molly steps out the door, nearly tripping over the woman's loafered foot.

I rush to the door to help Molly since this bitch has no intention of doing so. When Molly sees me, her eyebrows shoot up and a faint smile materializes on her slack, drunken features. Molly is such a pretty girl. I've only been to Tristan's house once, a couple of years ago for Molly's birthday party, but she has the same glossy, light-brown hair as Tristan. She doesn't have Tristan's gray eyes. Her eyes are a golden brown, muddied now by the haze of alcohol. This was me last year, before I met Eddie and stopped drinking so much. I hate the fact that that controlling, manipulative asshole is responsible for anything positive in my life.

'Carissa is sleeping off the whiskey, in case you were wondering,' the frizzy-haired woman proclaims as I grab Molly's arm to hold her upright.

'I'm very sorry about this. I don't know how they could have gotten the alcohol. I mean, it couldn't have been here, in this house, could it?' I reply with as much phony concern as I can stomach.

Frizzball narrows her eyes at me. 'She's not allowed back here, ever again.'

'Well, she'll be devastated to hear you're closing the open bar. But I'm sure she'll get her fix somewhere else.' Molly doubles over as she cackles at my response and I wrap my arm around her waist to keep her from toppling over. 'Come on, girl. Your brother is waiting for you.'

Molly's left hand latches onto my coat and we hobble down the long walkway toward Tristan's car. We're a few feet away when she begins to retch. I scoot back to get out of her way and maybe grab her hair to hold it back, but I don't step out of the way fast enough and her watery vomit splashes over my shoe and the pavement.

'Sorry,' she mutters before another stream of vomit spews forth.

This time I'm able to pull her hair back and take safety behind her as she finishes. It must be fifty degrees out here, but her face is red and sweaty and I'm not looking forward to riding home in Tristan's fancy car with the stench of vomit wafting up from my foot. I help Molly into the car and her head flops to the side as I buckle her seatbelt. I take off my shoes and spend about five minutes looking for the button to pop the trunk. I throw my heels in the trunk then I slide into the driver's seat and head back.

We're nearly there when Molly mumbles something I almost wish I didn't understand. 'I hate my life.'

I wait until we're stopped at Hillsborough and Dixie Trail before I say anything. 'Do you want to go straight home or do you want to go somewhere and sober up first?'

'I don't want to go home like this.'

'That's what I thought. We'll go hang out for a little while.'

I drive her to a local burger joint and order her some French fries so she can get something in her stomach. I text Tristan to tell him we're grabbing a bite to eat, then we sit in the parking lot as she nibbles the fries and I wait for her to say something.

'Are you Claire's friend?' she finally asks.

'Her very best friend.'

'I miss Claire,' she whispers. 'Don't tell Tristan I said that. I said it in front of him a few weeks ago and he got pissed.'

He probably got pissed because, according to bro-code, you're automatically supposed to hate the girl who broke your friend's heart. Of course, Tristan probably doesn't know the whole story behind Chris and Claire's breakup. I probably don't even know the full story. And this animosity Tristan holds for Claire only reminds me that there is one more obstacle standing in the way of Tristan and me – the truth. I don't know Tristan very well. He doesn't know me or my best friend. And there's no denying it, Claire is my fucking soul sister. I can't be with a guy who doesn't love and respect her.

'I won't say a word. Do you want to talk about anything else?'

She shakes her head and sets the bag of French fries

on the floor of the car next to her feet. 'I want to go home.'

When I pull into the driveway of Tristan's grandma's house, he's sitting on the front steps waiting for us. He gets to his feet quickly and immediately heads for the passenger door to help Molly.

'Are you sick?' he asks and she shakes her head, though I can see she's still swaying a bit as she walks around the car and toward the front door.

Tristan attempts to grab her arm to help her, but she pushes him away. 'Leave me alone. I don't want to talk to you.'

He looks at me for some kind of explanation, but all I can do is shrug. 'I should get going,' I proclaim as I retrieve my heels from the trunk.

'Did she say anything to you?'

'Not really. She's just upset. You should try to talk to her . . . She needs you.'

He looks at me as if he's seeing me for the first time tonight, then he reaches forward and I try not to flinch as he touches the backs of his fingers to my abdomen. 'We still need to talk about this, don't we?'

I take a step back so I'm out of his reach. 'I'll call you when I'm done studying this weekend.'

I turn to leave, but he grabs my hand. 'Happy Thanksgiving.'

Chapter Twelve

Nine Years Ago

The windows of the rundown duplex on Clover Lane all glow with various shades of yellow light at 2.30 a.m. Not that I didn't expect Elaine's house to be jumping at this hour, but it still makes me nervous about what I'll find in there.

I rode my bike to Elaine's place in Southeast Raleigh all the way from West Raleigh. Grandma doesn't know I'm gone. She thinks I'm sleeping at my friend Noah's house right now, but I *had* to leave.

I'm twelve years old. I've spent the last two years helping Grandma train Molly to piss in a toilet. Before that I was changing diapers; waking up in the middle of the night to quiet Molly down whenever Grandma wasn't feeling well from her migraines; waking up early on Saturdays so Grandma could go to the farmer's market where she insists everything is cheaper. I'm tired of that shit. And now she doesn't want to let me quit school to get a job. I don't get it. She's the one always complaining about not having any money and she won't even let me help. She only needs me for the dirty jobs.

But that's not the reason I'm leaving.

I didn't want to come here to Elaine's, but she's the only one I know who won't turn me away. Why would she? They take anyone and everyone in here: crack-heads, prostitutes, murderers. I lived with Elaine until I was nine and Molly was one, when we moved here to Raleigh from Maine. After that girl did those things to me in the ice-cream shop, I lied to Grandma and told her I found a needle in Molly's playpen. I didn't think she would report Elaine. I never told Grandma what happened at the ice-cream shop. I never had to. I never saw that blonde girl again.

I roll my bike behind a box hedge to hide it, then I knock on the door. My heart pounds against my chest like a crackhead on a dealer's front door, which is probably what they think I am. The door opens and I freeze when I see the shotgun pointed at my face.

'Who the fuck are you?' an old guy covered in tattoos demands.

'I'm – I'm here for Elaine.'

He narrows his eyes and his leathery skin crinkles at the edges. 'What the fuck do you want with her?'

'Who is it?' Elaine's voice makes me cringe inside, but there must be relief on my face because the guy lowers the shotgun a little.

'She's my . . .' – *gulp* – '. . . my mom.'

The guy smiles, but only with the left side of his face, as he lowers the gun to his side and opens the screen door separating us. 'Well, come on in, son.' I tuck my hands into the front pockets of my hoodie as I step inside so he can't see that I'm still shaking. 'Don't worry. I ain't your daddy,' he says with a laugh as he closes the door.

I shouldn't have come here, but what other choice do I have? When I went to Noah's house this afternoon, all the watches we stole from the kiosk in the mall were laid out on his kitchen table. His mom had left a note saying that she had gone to pick up Noah's little sister and we were to wait for her until she got back. There was almost $2,000 in watches staring me in the face and I knew that I couldn't stick around to see what kind of punishment Noah's mom had planned for us. Even if she didn't call the police, I knew she'd at least make us return the watches; and what if the owner of the kiosk called the police? It would break Grandma's heart to know that I fucked up so badly.

Fuck Noah and his bitch mom.

I'll call Grandma in the morning to let her know I'm going to stay with Elaine for a few weeks, until school starts, so she doesn't send out a search party. Then I'm going to make some cash at Elaine's and get myself a motorcycle. Then I can quit school, get a job, and go anywhere. I can help Grandma with money and maybe she'll forgive me for stealing those watches.

I stand next to the grimy blue sofa, unsure whether I should sit since I wasn't offered a seat. The sound of footsteps is quickly followed by Elaine's entrance in a T-shirt that barely covers the tops of her legs. She's smoking a cigarette and her dark hair is pulled up in a messy bun that hangs over the back of her neck.

'What are you doing here? It's almost three o'clock in the morning.'

'I need some money. I just need a place to stay for a few weeks until I can make some money for a motorcycle.'

She cocks one of her thin eyebrows as if I've asked her to go to a fucking PTA meeting with me. 'So you came *here*?' I nod and she's overtaken by a bout of shrill laughter. 'Well, I'll be . . . Mom is going to love this.' She takes a moment to compose herself, then she asks, 'Why don't you just get a summer job? It's not so . . . illegal.'

'School starts next week. I don't want to go back.' *It's also my birthday next week. August 27. Do you even remember that?*

She shrugs and nods toward the hallway. 'Come get some blankets so you can make up a bed on the couch. Tomorrow, we'll put you to work.'

Chapter Thirteen

After Senia blew me off last weekend in favor of studying, I didn't expect her to come over tonight. She claims she still has a lot of studying to do, but Claire is out of the dorm for a Friday-night birthday dinner with Chris and Jackie. This is her opportunity to sneak out undetected.

I get why she doesn't want Claire to find out about the pregnancy. I'm not a complete asshole. I don't want Chris to find out either. But she won't be able to hide it for long. We need to discuss this – and I need to get her alone – soon.

When I open my front door, I'm not surprised to see her in jeans. She thinks the extra clothing will deter me.

'Welcome to my not-so-humble abode.'

'This house is way too big for one person,' she says as she turns her back to me so I can take her coat.

I slip the coat off and hang it up in the coat closet as she glances around the foyer at the marble floors, the sweeping curved staircase, and the enormous industrial-era chandelier.

'You want something to drink?' I ask as I take a few steps toward the kitchen, hoping she'll follow me instead of standing there with her mouth agape.

'The only thing that's missing in here is a ten-foot-tall self-portrait.'

'That's in the study.'

She turns to me and purses her lips. 'Exactly how rich are you?'

'I'm not rich. I'm wealthy.'

She sighs as she follows me into the kitchen. I open the refrigerator and pull out a bottle of water. When I turn around to hand it to her, she's too busy admiring the glossy white cabinets to notice. I press the cold bottle against the back of her neck and she gasps as she steps aside.

'You bastard!' she cries. I chuckle as I hold the bottle out to her and she waits a moment before she takes it. 'You're a child. How the hell are you able to live here by yourself without setting the house on fire?'

'Baby, this house has been set on fire multiple times.'

'Ugh. You are such a player,' she groans, holding her hands out as I approach her. 'Don't touch me.'

'That won't last long.'

'Are we talking about your erection?'

I chuckle as her hands press against my chest. 'Your humor only turns me on even more.'

She pushes me hard and quickly scoots sideways to

get away from me. 'We need to talk,' she says as she scurries around the kitchen island and takes a seat at the breakfast bar with her bottle of water. 'I'm scared shitless.'

'I can help you with that.'

'With what?' she whispers breathlessly as I stand behind the barstool and brush her ponytail aside.

'All of it. If you want to talk, we'll talk.' I kiss the back of her neck and the plastic water bottle in her handle crackles as she tightens her grip. 'If you want to keep the baby, I'll be there. Anything you need' – I spin the barstool around so she's facing me – 'I can give it to you.'

I lean in and she whimpers as I brush my lips softly over hers.

'Don't do this.'

'Why?' I whisper, then I slide my tongue into her mouth so she doesn't have a chance to respond.

She tastes like orange Tic Tacs. Grabbing her face, I kiss her slowly as she grips my forearms. I suck on her luscious bottom lip and she wraps one of her long legs around me.

She turns her face away and shakes her head. 'Stop. We have to talk.'

I sigh and try not to look too disappointed as I take a step back. 'Let's talk.'

'You said you'd give me anything I need,' she says, and the tough, sarcastic exterior she usually wears so well is peeled back for a moment. 'I need to talk about this.'

Her brown eyes search mine for a sign of understanding, but I'm just frustrated. 'Do you mind if I have a beer while we talk?'

I'm not sure why I'm asking her permission other than I don't want to hear a snide remark or see her roll her eyes when I grab the beer out of the fridge.

'This is your domain. Don't let me stop you.'

'You kind of just did that,' I remark as I take a step back, but she grabs the front of my Vandals T-shirt.

Before I can even question what she's doing, my shirt is off and my hands are under her sweater, roaming over her soft, warm flesh. Her breasts feel bigger than the last time we fucked, and this instantly gets me hard. I kiss her neck as I move my hands down to grab hold of her ass. Then I scoot her forward on the barstool, so she can feel me hard against her.

'I don't want to fuck you here,' I murmur into her ear.

'Why?' she whimpers as she reaches for the button on my jeans.

'Because I have something so much better planned for you.'

I grab her hand and lead her toward the French doors that lead out onto the patio and outdoor dining area. Just beyond and to the right of the dining area is an Olympic-length saltwater pool and jacuzzi.

'If you think I'm getting in the jacuzzi with you when it's fifty degrees out here, you've got another thing coming.'

'Shh. We're almost there,' I say as we pass the pool and the outdoor shower area. Finally, we reach a cedar-plank door in the rear corner of the house. I reach into my back pocket to pull out the door key and she shakes her head.

'You knew you'd get me back here.'

I smile as I turn the key in the lock and push the door open to the steam room. I left the lights on and put the steam going before she got here. I've had other girls in here. It's nothing new to me. But I've yet to meet a girl who wasn't pleasantly surprised by the overwhelmingly hot experience of sex in a steam room.

'I'm not having sex with you in a steam room. I've done it before and I nearly suffocated. I don't want to know what will happen if I try to do it while pregnant.'

'Shit. I didn't think about that. But, wait a minute, you've had sex in a steam room? When?'

'Uh . . . how is that any of your business?'

Closing the door to the steam room, I clench my jaw as I attempt to bite back my response. If a girl isn't being needy and clingy, she's playing hard-to-get. Why can't they just chill out and enjoy the offer of commitment-free sex?

'Why do you look like I just crashed your car?' she asks as she follows me back to the patio. 'I didn't say we can't have sex. I just said we can't have sex in the steam room. And, really, that's just common sense.'

'Common sense?' I repeat this as I hold the patio door open for her to enter the great room.

'Yeah. I mean, why would I want to have sex in a steam room when I nearly passed out while throwing up this morning?'

'You what?' I bark this question at her and she appears startled.

'I was sick this morning before I got a chance to eat anything. I was dry-heaving so badly that I felt like I was going to pass out. It's no big deal. I took a ten-minute nap in the dorm after Claire left for class.'

'No big deal? Don't you think you should talk to your doctor about that? Have you even seen a doctor yet?'

'Fuck no! I'm still on my parents' health insurance and they can't know anything until we figure out what we're gonna do.'

I try not to let her see the conflicting emotions and thoughts racing through my mind right now. I want to offer to pay for her doctor visit out of my own pocket, but I also want to hold off. This is a card I may want to hold on to so I can play it later when I lay down my whole hand.

I take a seat on the gray sofa in the living room and pat the seat for her to join me. 'Can't you go to the campus health center and get a free exam? Shouldn't you be taking vitamins or something?'

She narrows her eyes at me as she sits. 'Are you trying to tell me you want me to keep it?'

Her words make my breath hitch in my chest. The truth is I'm probably more prepared to take care of this baby than Senia. But being prepared doesn't mean I'll be any good at it. The last thing I need is to screw up my own kid the way I've obviously screwed up Molly. I had to pick her up from school early yesterday. She was suspended for cutting class two days in a row so she could smoke weed with her innocent friend Carissa at the park. It's always the kids with the most clueless parents that seem to get into the most trouble. Maybe if I had been there for Molly this past year, none of this would be happening. I'm not ready to be a father.

But I don't think I can pass up this opportunity. This is my chance to send Grandma off with a full heart. Who knows? She may even live long enough to meet her great-grandchild. I don't think anything would make me happier than that.

'Yes. If you want to keep it, so do I.'

Chapter Fourteen

After a moment of awkward silence, I grab the remote and turn on the TV. 'What do you want to watch?'

She stares at the TV for a moment as the picture materializes, then she turns to me. 'I should get going. Claire will probably be getting back from dinner soon.'

'Did Claire-bear give you a curfew?'

'I don't want her to ask me where I was tonight.'

I'm used to being a dirty secret. I've had affairs with plenty of girls, and women, who were otherwise attached. But this just pisses me off. There are very few things about my personal life that I feel comfortable sharing with anyone. But this . . . This is something I want to share, like a fucking Circle of Life moment, I want to shout it from the mountaintops. I made a *human*.

I've watched way too many Disney movies with Moon.

'Why are you wearing jeans today?' I ask so I don't have to address the issue of when we'll be sharing the news of our lovechild with our BFFs.

'It's cold.'

'Can I tell you a story?'

She looks at me as if I've asked her if I could tap-dance for her. 'Okay . . .'

I clear my throat and smile. 'I was eight when Molly was born. I was still living with . . . with my mom.' Senia doesn't need to know that I only refer to her as Elaine. 'I was still living in Maine with my mom.' Man, it feels weird to call her my mom. 'We were living in a shitty apartment in South Portland and I hadn't slept the whole night, waiting for my mom to come home with Molly.'

'Who was with you?'

'No one,' I reply without thinking, and she looks at me with a sad look that I'm all too familiar with. 'It's not like it was the first time I had spent the night alone.' This doesn't make the concerned look on Senia's face dissipate, so I continue before she can ask any more questions. 'Anyway, when my mom came home with Molly, I finally fell asleep on the floor next to her bassinet. I think that was one of the happiest moments of my life. So . . .'

Her eyebrows are scrunched together awaiting the next words out of my mouth. 'So . . . *what*?'

'So . . . I think I know why Chris and Claire got back together. And I think I want to tell them about the baby . . . soon.'

'Oh.' She puts her feet up on the coffee table and sits back as she contemplates this. 'I just don't know how she's going to feel about it. And you should be worried about how Chris is going to take it. From what I've gathered, he is hanging all his hopes on this whole open adoption thing. If he finds out you're having a kid . . .'

'It will kill him.'

For the last few months, Chris and Claire have been embroiled in negotiations with the adoptive parents of Abigail, the daughter Claire gave up for adoption earlier this year. I still don't understand how Chris could forgive Claire for doing something like that without giving him any choice in the matter. I know he thinks she did it so he wouldn't cancel the tour and give up on his dreams, but I don't think I'd be as forgiving in his place.

'Do you want to kill your best friend?' she asks.

'Maybe it will help him to think that I know a little about what he's going through.'

Before Senia can respond, her hip twitches and she pulls her phone out of her jeans pocket.

'Who is it?' I ask. Not that I have a right to ask, but I can pretend I do.

'It's Claire,' she says. 'She's spending the night at Chris's condo. Chris has a condo?'

I shrug, even though I already knew this. He told me about it a couple of days ago after he and Claire got back together. 'That means you can stay the night here,' I murmur as I reach over and tuck her dark hair behind her ear.

She scoots farther away from me and shakes her head. 'No, it doesn't. I still don't know what time she's coming back to the dorm in the morning.'

She grins at me as if this is just an invitation for me to convince her to stay a little longer, even if she doesn't stay the night. 'Yeah, maybe you should just go.' I don't need to tell her that I always have breakfast with Chris on Saturday mornings. It's a tradition that began after he broke up with Claire and we stopped doing the usual breakfast with the band on Sundays.

'Are you telling me to leave?'

I stand from the sofa and smile as I hold out my hand to help her up. 'You should probably go so you don't fall asleep in my bed and your whole secret is blown wide open when Claire sees your empty bed in the morning.'

'Fall asleep in your bed?' She takes my hand and allows me to pull her up from the sofa. Our noses are centimeters apart when she replies. 'What makes you think you can even get me into your bed?' She shakes my hand loose and heads for the foyer. 'I guess we'll break the news to them sometime before Christmas. Until then, I'd appreciate it if you could keep this to yourself, and . . . I'll let you know how the exam goes at the health center.'

'Thanks,' I mutter. Then in one swift motion, I take her face in my hands and plant a soft kiss on her cheekbone. 'Drive safe.'

*

Sliding my leg off my bike, I pull my phone out of my pocket and check the screen. It's the first thing I do when I come off my motorcycle and the text I find makes me grin. Chris texted me a few minutes ago to say that Senia and Claire will be joining us at the pancake house this morning. I want to know what they had to do to get Senia to come here.

I tuck the phone into my back pocket and hang my helmet from the seat hook. Then I lean back against the bike and wait. An entire breakfast with Senia attempting to keep the baby a secret from Claire and Chris. This should be interesting.

When Senia arrives, she looks pissed, as if she's been forced to come here, and she ignores me until we're seated at the semicircular booth. When Chris and Claire both guess each other's breakfast orders, I try to make a cute guess about what Senia will be ordering.

'Hey, I'll bet I can guess what you're ordering,' I say to Senia. 'The *stuffed* French toast.'

She looks up from her menu and turns to Claire. 'Do you hear someone talking to me?'

'You heard me loud and clear last night,' I reply with a grin.

Claire looks up from her menu. 'What is he talking about?'

Senia finally looks in my direction and the glare she's pointing at me could slice me in half. But, somehow, it's not Senia's glare that gets to me. It's the subtle outrage in Claire's question.

I've always tried to keep my feelings about Claire to myself. When she and Chris were together the first time, before we went on tour last year, I managed to keep my comments about Chris being whipped to a minimum. The truth is I've always kind of envied what Chris and Claire have, though I'll never admit that to anyone. But it's not really the love that I envy, it's the trust. The feeling that no matter how bad you screw up, there is always someone who will accept you and love you for who you are; not because they have to, just because they can't *not* love you.

I thought I had that with Ashley, but it turns out I didn't know shit about her. You can believe you're destined for someone – you can share the most gut-wrenchingly intimate experience with someone – and still not know a damn thing about them. And there is irony in learning that you can't trust someone you love because it makes you stop trusting yourself.

The waitress arrives in time to ease the tension and take our food order. Once she's gone, Chris whispers something in Claire's ear and I find myself glancing at Senia's hand, itching to grab it and announce our secret.

Suddenly, I realize Chris and Claire are having a discussion about living together over breakfast and right in front of Senia and me.

'Of course I want to live with you,' Claire continues, 'but are you sure you want to live with me?'

'Wait a minute,' Senia interrupts their conversation. 'Are you moving out?'

It's as if Senia and I – and this entire restaurant – don't exist, the way Chris and Claire gaze into each other's eyes. 'I've never been more sure of anything,' he replies.

Claire grins hugely as she turns to Senia. 'I guess I'm moving out, but not until the end of the semester.'

'That's eleven days away,' Senia pouts. 'I have eleven days to find another roomie?'

'I'll pay your housing for the next semester,' Chris offers. 'Not just Claire's half. I'll pay it all.'

'You don't have to do that. I'll pay it,' I say, watching Senia for her response, but her eyes are locked on Claire.

'It's not the money,' Senia insists. 'My dad will cover Claire's half.'

All I can do is watch in silence as Claire contemplates her options. 'I don't want to leave you alone,' she says to Senia.

After everything Senia and I discussed last night, I just want to yell at her to put Claire out of her misery. I wait a moment before I open my mouth to say something, but Senia beats me to it. 'I'm pregnant.'

Claire is frozen, stunned, for a moment before she looks back and forth between Senia and me. 'How? You and Eddie have been broken up for three months.'

Ugh. I can't stand that guy's name. Sounds like a fucking sleazy truck driver.

Senia's shoulders slump as she shrinks in her seat. 'It's not Eddie's.'

Claire is confused until Senia nods toward me. 'When? What the hell's going on?'

'I'm sorry. I didn't want to tell you because of everything going on with Abigail,' Senia continues. 'It was just a one-night thing a few weeks ago and we were careful, but I didn't get my period last week.'

She just lied to Claire and said we used protection. I try not to laugh out loud at this.

'Wait a minute. A few weeks ago?' Claire replies. 'Thanksgiving was two weeks ago. I thought you were going to tell him to stop texting you.'

'We ran into each other at Yogurtland and it just sort of happened. I didn't give him my number. I mean, I'm not *stupid*.'

'Hey!' I interject. 'How about a little gratitude for the guy whose seed is sprouting inside of you?'

'Ew,' Senia replies without looking at me. 'That's why I was wondering how he got my number and texted me on Thanksgiving. I'm sorry I didn't tell you about it, but I was ashamed of myself for giving in. I was feeling so shitty because Eddie kept texting and calling. I just wanted to do something to take my mind off of him.'

I suppress my feelings about hearing his trashy name as I softly lay my hand on the back of her neck. 'There's nothing to be ashamed of, sweetheart.'

As expected, she pushes my hand off. 'Stop it.'

I smile as I lean back, but the look on Chris's face quickly wipes the smile off mine. He looks like he did the day he ran into Claire at the Pour House in downtown Raleigh; the day he found out that Claire had been keeping the worst kind of secret a person can keep from him. He shoots up from the table and heads for the exit.

I stand up to go after him, but Claire puts her hand out to stop me. 'Not now.'

Watching her chase after Chris, I try not to get upset when I realize that Chris needs her more than he needs his best friend. He always has.

I take a seat in the booth and Senia is looking at me with an expression on her face that looks slightly like admiration. 'What?'

She smiles and sighs softly. 'You're a good friend.'

I roll my eyes because this topic makes me feel uncomfortable. No one – not even Chris – knows that he basically saved me from a life of crime and drugs when he asked me if I wanted to start a band.

'No, don't do that. Don't belittle it. You're a good friend,' she insists, then she closes her eyes and takes a deep breath before she continues. 'And you'll make a great father.'

I stare at the table for a moment, lost in thoughts of what it will be like to hold a human being that I made in my hands. I can write a song and I can play it until my fingers bleed, but I can't carry music in my hands. I can't touch it or smell it. I can't give it my heart.

I look up and her gaze meets mine. 'Move in with me. Let me take care of you.'

Her mouth hangs open at the sound of my words. I reach forward and lift her chin with my finger to close her mouth. She pulls my hand away from her chin and I smile as her mouth drops open again.

'I . . . I don't think that's a good idea.'

'Why? I'm not far from campus and you won't have to worry about telling your parents about the baby until you're ready.'

'Not far from campus? You're at least thirty minutes from UNC. Besides, living with you is not something I would consider a smart decision.'

'I'm not asking you to move in so we can have worry-free sex all day long. I'm asking because you need someone to take care of you now that Claire is moving out.'

'Can you *ever* be serious? Is that really your best attempt at convincing me to move in with you?'

I reach forward and she flinches a little as I take her hand. 'You need to stop being so stuck in your head and just learn to go with the flow. We all know you're smart and independent. We get it. How about you show us you're willing to let go of your pride and do whatever it takes for your baby?' She looks slightly offended by this, so I add one more bit of information in my attempt to convince her. 'I promise to keep my hands to myself . . . if you do.'

She chews on her bottom lip as she contemplates this proposal. It takes everything in me not to brush her hair aside and kiss those lips. Finally, she smiles. 'You like me.'

'What?'

'I see the way you're looking at me. You don't just want my golden egg. You want the whole goose. You. Like. Me.'

I chuckle at this comparison. 'I'm not sure if you're referring to the baby or your pussy as a golden egg, but, either way, let's keep this to ourselves. Yes, I want you. Yes, I . . . *like* you.'

She shakes her head, but she's still smiling. 'Okay. I'll move in with you.'

Chapter Fifteen

I lie awake the whole night wondering if I've gotten myself into something that will undo me. I've never lived with a girlfriend – not that Senia's my girlfriend. Yet. I've lived with Molly and Grandma most of my life, so I know about all the weird and gross things girls do in the privacy of their homes, but I've never actually lived with someone who wasn't related to me – unless you count the summer before seventh grade when I lived with Elaine, but I never count that.

By the time I show up at Grandma's house at 9 a.m. on Sunday morning, I'm having trouble keeping my eyes open. Entering the house, I'm greeted by the clanging of dishes in the kitchen. I close the door softly then head for the kitchen to surprise her.

The sight of her washing the breakfast dishes makes me sad. She shouldn't have to do any cleaning during the last months of her life. I'm hiring her a maid tomorrow.

'Grandma?'

She whips her head around at the sound of my voice and she sighs with relief. 'Oh, I'm so happy to see you.'

I give her a hug and a kiss on the cheek before I take a seat at the breakfast table. 'Why are you so happy to see me?'

She sighs again, but this time it's a heavy sigh weighed down by something I'm sure I don't want to hear. 'Molly came home late last night and she was drunk. I'm so worried about her. I tried to talk to her and tell her that we still have a lot of time to be together, but she was so out of it when I put her to bed. I don't know if she heard anything I said. She's still sleeping. I want to give her some time to sleep it off before I try to talk to her again.'

'I'll talk to her,' I offer, gritting my teeth against the sudden urge I have to barge into Molly's room and shake some sense into her. 'It's my fault she thinks it's okay to do that. I'll take care of it.'

'It's not your fault.'

'Don't worry about it; just sit down,' I say, grabbing her hand as she reaches for a clean towel to dry the dishes she just washed. She purses her lips as I pull her away from the sink so she can sit at the table with me. 'I have some news for you.'

'Well, it better be good. I'm not sure how much more bad news a woman in my condition can take.'

'It's better than good.' I keep a tight grip on her hand as I lean forward on my elbows and look her in the eye. 'I'm having a baby.'

Her eyebrows scrunch up and I can't tell if she's confused or if she's going to cry. 'Are you pulling my leg, because this is not funny?'

'No, I'm not joking. Are you not happy?'

She swallows hard and then the tears come and she quickly covers her face.

'Grandma, are you okay?'

She nods her head as she reaches for a napkin in the center of the table. She dabs the corners of her eyes and I start to worry that maybe I was wrong. Maybe she doesn't want me to have a baby. Maybe she thinks I'm not ready.

What the fuck was I thinking? Of course she thinks I'm not ready.

She stops wiping at her face with the napkin, even though her eyes are still tearing. 'When?'

I let out a small sigh. 'Not for a while. She's only a few weeks along. But I know you can make it.' My voice sounds garbled as my throat begins to close. 'I know you're gonna be there when it happens.'

She smiles weakly and grabs my hand. 'I'm just so scared of leaving you all behind. The thought of leaving behind one more person . . .'

'I didn't mean to upset you.'

'I know,' she replies quickly as she leans forward and stares at the surface of the table. 'I think the depression is setting in. The doctor said it would come soon and to prepare myself for it, but I don't even know how to be prepared for this.' She squeezes her eyes shut and I reach forward to grab her hand. 'It just hit me so hard. I feel like I don't know what to do with myself any more. My mind just goes in circles all day and I find myself in a different room of the house, not sure how or why I'm there.'

I've never seen Grandma Flo like this. It kills me to think that the last months of her life will be spent worrying about the people she's leaving behind.

'I'm going to take care of Molly and the baby. Don't you worry about them.'

'And the girl?'

'Who?'

'I know you never bring girls here any more, but I'd like to meet the girl who's going to be the mother of my great-grandchild. I'd like to think you're going to take care of her, too.' She fixes me with a stern look and I can't help but smile.

'You've already met her.' She looks surprised, so I continue before she can question me. 'It's Senia, Claire's best friend. She came over a few years ago for Molly's birthday.'

'I don't remember her.'

'Well, when you meet her again you'll never forget her.'

She pulls my hand to her chest and hugs it as if it's a precious gift. 'Thank you for coming here to tell me. When are you bringing her over?'

'Actually, she was here last week while you were asleep.' I take a deep breath and brace myself for the inevitable regret that will come from speaking the words I'm about to say. 'But she's moving in with me next weekend. Do you think you might want to come over with Molly?'

'To . . . to your house?'

I get a sharp pain in my chest at the sight of her uncertainty. I wish I didn't have to keep my address a secret from Grandma and Molly – they're just too easily influenced by Elaine. But I can't keep being so cautious. I need to show Grandma and Moon that I trust them.

'Yeah, to my house. Senia or I will pick you both up next Saturday. Is that okay?'

'Is that okay? Oh, Tristan, that is not just okay. Those are the most beautiful words I've heard in months. I can't wait to see your house. I'm . . .' She pauses to collect herself. 'I'm so proud of you. You know that, don't you? Everything you've done this year. You've made me so proud. And now this . . . You've made me the happiest old woman in the world.'

I smile as I realize that this news has done exactly what I wanted it to do. It's given Grandma a small thread of hope that she can hold on to for the next few months. I only hope that Molly will feel the same way.

I arrive at the pub at 7.15 p.m., just as Link is setting out two frosty pints of beer in front of Chris. As usual, Chris is sitting in the last seat at the end of the bar. When he sees me, he throws me a curt nod. He's still not over what happened at the pancake house.

'Hey, man,' I mutter as I take a seat next to him. 'Is this Pliny?'

'What else would it be?'

We sit in silence for probably five minutes, but it feels like an hour. I don't know if there's anything I can say to Chris that would make this situation less awkward. Then he says something that makes me feel even more awful.

'They blew us off. There won't be an open adoption. We got the letter this morning.'

'Fuck. I'm sorry, man. I don't know what to say. I thought that telling you about . . . about Senia was the right thing to do. I fucked up.'

'Why? It's not like . . .'

I have a feeling he was about to say, *It's not like you can keep the pregnancy a secret.* We all know that's not true. Chris and Claire are living proof of what happens when you hide a pregnancy.

'It doesn't matter,' Chris continues, then takes a long swig of his beer. 'It's over. Abigail isn't going to know us. But it's just the beginning for you two. Don't do what I did. Don't fuck it up.'

I stare at the rising bubbles in my glass as I try to absorb these words. 'I won't.'

Chapter Sixteen

Senia

I can't believe I'm moving off-campus . . . *for a guy!* What have I become? Eddie asked me to move in with him at least a dozen times over the summer and I never caved. Just once was all it took from Tristan's oh-so-suckable lips and now I'm glancing around my cleaned-out dorm room to see if I've forgotten anything. There is no hope for me.

I throw an almost-empty bottle of pear-scented hand lotion into the waste bin then I sit on the edge of my bed and lie back to stare at the ceiling. Claire walks in and smiles as she catches me rubbing my belly, but I can see the months of regret etched in that smile as well as the weariness from this past week she's spent grieving the loss of Abigail.

'Tristan and Chris should be done unloading everything in an hour. Want to grab a bite to eat on the way there? You must be hungry after all that packing.'

I want to tell her it's not fair that I get to have a baby just as she and Chris have lost theirs, but I don't want to slow any progress she's made since she received the news on Sunday. The open adoption they had their hearts set on is not going to happen. They will never have a chance to know the daughter Claire gave up for adoption in April unless, by some merciful twist of fate, the adoptive parents change their minds or their daughter decides to track them down when she turns eighteen. I can't even imagine what it must feel like to lose a child whose body you've snuggled in your arms, whose name you've whispered in your sleep.

'How about we just lie here and talk about boys? For old times' sake.'

She lies down next to me and I hook my arm in hers as we stare at the ceiling and talk about everything we've been too busy to talk about for the past few weeks. She gives me all the gritty details about the first night she spent with Chris a couple of weeks ago and I tell her about the brief, yet satisfying, conversation I had with Eddie a few days ago where I told him to 'delete my number from your phone and try to slam your tiny cock in a heavy door'. When the conversation runs thin, we head over to Tristan's house in Cary – *my* home in Cary.

Chris and Claire don't hang around because she has too much studying to do, and I don't know why Chris thinks this is so funny, so we say our goodbyes out on the curved driveway then I head back into the house. I find Tristan upstairs, ripping the tape off my moving boxes.

'Are you going to unpack my things, too?' I ask as I take a seat on the low platform bed in this guest room. Tristan's house has five bedrooms and eight bathrooms. That's just ridiculous.

He glances at me over his shoulder as I lie back and his gaze slides over me, pausing a bit too long at my chest. 'Which box has the stuff from your goodie drawer?'

I laugh and the sly grin on his face makes my heart stutter. 'There'll be none of that,' I say, grabbing a fluffy white pillow and hugging it to hide my chest. 'I need to unpack and study. Get out of here.'

'Don't you want to shower?'

For a moment, I can't breathe as I imagine Tristan naked and dripping wet. I shake my head to loosen the image then I stand from the bed. 'Actually, yes, I'd love to take a shower.' I grab my make-up case and my handbag where I stuffed a plastic bag containing all my toiletries. 'I know where the bathroom is.'

He grabs the back of my T-shirt before I can leave the bedroom. 'You can use the shower in the master bath. It's much bigger.'

I wriggle away from him and step aside so he can lead me to the master bedroom. My pulse is pounding in every part of my body as I follow him down the hallway and into a bedroom so huge I'm certain I could fit six dorm rooms in here. He leads me past the modern furnishings and I discreetly glance inside his walk-in closet. It's a little messy, but there's definitely enough room in there for my clothes.

Stop it, Senia!

'Why are you grinning?' he asks me as we enter the master bathroom.

'No reason. Just excited to get clean and get some studying done.'

He shows me how to turn on the shower and he stays until he's certain the water is the right temperature. 'The handheld shower-head has a pulse-mode,' he says with a wink.

As soon as I'm cleaned up and changed into something that doesn't smell like the inside of our ancient closet in the dorm, I make my way downstairs with my book bag and my cell phone. I pull my laptop out of the bag and sit back on the sofa in the living room to get some work done. I don't know where Tristan is, but I don't have time to care.

My phone rings as I'm opening my laptop and I'm not at all surprised to see it's Tristan. 'What?'

'Want to play hide-and-seek?'

'Very funny.'

'I'm serious. I'll let you hide first. The refrigerator is home base. I'll count to thirty.'

He hangs up and I roll my eyes as I try to think of a good reason to play hide-and-seek with Tristan that has nothing to do with sex. Finally, I close my laptop and set it down on the coffee table.

I don't know my way around this huge house very well yet, but I guess a game of hide-and-seek should help with that. I have no idea where Tristan is, so I set off toward the kitchen. I'm thinking I should try to hide somewhere downstairs – somewhere far away from the bedrooms. I open a glass door that looks like it leads to a cellar, when suddenly I hear the sound of a door opening. I scurry inside and close the door softly behind me.

Dashing down the steps, I reach the bottom and find a warmly lit wine cellar with a few barrels in the corner. I crouch down behind one of the barrels and realize, not only is my heart pounding with the anticipation of being discovered, I'm grinning like a crazy person. The sound of footsteps on the wooden stairs has me frozen. I cover my mouth to muffle the sound of my frantic breathing.

'Are you hiding in my cellar?' Tristan's smooth voice sends a chill over my skin.

I try to make myself even smaller, but it's hard to do that when you're almost six feet tall without heels. His footsteps are getting closer. He lets out a soft chuckle and I'm certain he's found me, but many years of playing hide-and-seek with my sisters taught me that you never come out of your hiding place until someone taps your shoulder. Never assume you've been caught.

I wait another thirty seconds, my eyes squeezed

tightly shut, until the sound of footsteps traveling up the staircase surprises me. Opening my eyes, I slowly lean my head to the side to peek around the barrel. He's gone.

I want to laugh triumphantly, but I have to make my dash for the refrigerator as quickly and quietly as possible. I creep up the stairs slowly, being careful not to step on any creaky stairs. At the top of the stairs, I peek in all directions beyond the glass door and see no movement. I burst through the door and just as I'm about to make a mad dash for the refrigerator, Tristan grabs me around the waist and I let out a wild scream.

'Got ya!' he says through his laughter as I attempt to push him away.

'That's not fair!' I squeal. 'You're supposed to tag me if you find me. You're not supposed to *ambush* me!'

'I couldn't resist. You really thought you'd picked a good hiding place.'

I sigh as I take a few steps away from him. 'Your turn to hide.'

He smiles at the sound of the challenge in my words. 'You're never going to find me.'

'We'll see about that.'

'Close your eyes,' he says and I reluctantly do as he says. I can't see anything, but I can feel the warmth of his breath on the side of my face. 'Don't forget to count to thirty.'

When thirty seconds is up, I open my eyes and head straight for the stairs. Something tells me I'm going to find Tristan naked in the shower – or maybe that's just wishful thinking. I search the master bedroom and bath and the entire second floor, but I come up with nothing. I search downstairs, even searching the cellar in case he decided to be cute, but he's nowhere. I head for the backyard and search behind the outdoor sofas, inside the pool supply closet. I even peer up inside the outdoor fireplace to see if I'll find Tristan propped up in there, covered in soot and looking sexy as ever. No such luck.

I walk past the pool, peering into the depths in case he's hiding under water. Then I realize I know where he is. I open the door to the steam room and Tristan is lying on the wooden bench with his eyes closed and his shirt off.

'You think you're so clever.'

He smiles as he opens his eyes. 'Oh, sorry. It was so cozy in here, I didn't hear you come in. Sure you don't want to join me?'

I can't help but stare at his rock-hard, glistening chest. This is what he wants. He wants me to give in to these urges and forget about my homework. Forget about everything else but him. And it would be so easy to get lost in Tristan.

'I have to study,' I say as I exit the steam room and he quickly follows after me. I grin as I imagine how cold it must feel out here to him after leaving the sauna with no shirt on. 'Next time you want to play hide-and-seek, call Chris.'

Chapter Seventeen

Nine Years Ago

I walk into the master bedroom at Elaine's house and I'm not surprised to find a girl lying spread-eagle on the bed wearing nothing but a black bra and panties. She looks young, maybe sixteen years old, with straight blonde hair that's fanned out over the pillow under her head.

'She's ready for you,' Elaine whispers from somewhere behind me. Maybe she's not whispering, but I can barely hear her over the blood rushing through my ears.

My gaze darts toward the corner where a fat guy in a T-shirt and jeans sits on a chair with his hand on his belt buckle, readying himself. I look back at the girl on the bed and I get an urge to know her name – this girl who's almost as young as I am and probably stuck in this impossible situation the same as I am. She closes her eyes, but she keeps them closed for a moment too long, and I know. I know she doesn't want to be here. She's probably saying a silent prayer to help her get through this.

I turn around and Elaine's gaunt face is contorted in confusion. 'What's wrong?'

'I can't do this.'

She grabs my arm before I can leave and whispers in my ear: 'How the fuck are we supposed to get out of here if you won't help me? I need you, Tristan. I need to get out of here.'

I glance over my shoulder and the blonde girl is staring at me now, looking a little rejected. 'I don't know how to do this.'

Elaine smiles softly. 'I'll show you how.'

Chapter Eighteen

Once Senia is settled in the study with her laptop and a phony sense of contempt for my games, I inform her that I'm leaving and I'll be back in about an hour. She looks a bit disappointed, but, again, she tries to cover this up with a casual goodbye. I hop in the Lightning and, I'll admit, I'm really excited about picking up Grandma and Molly. It would have been more convenient to have Senia pick them up on the way here, but I forgot that Claire's tiny car would probably be full of Senia's stuff. This is beyond all right because I'm dying to see Molly and Grandma's faces as we pull into the driveway.

When I arrive at Grandma's house, Molly and Grandma are standing outside under the darkening sky with their coats pulled tightly against the cold. Molly looks bored, but Grandma's face lights up the moment she sees my car. She must have forced Molly to wait outside with her.

'We are ready to be entertained,' Grandma declares

as she practically trots down the path toward the curb.

Molly rolls her eyes and I grab the back of her coat to pull her aside before she can climb into the backseat. 'Hey, I need you to not be in a mood today. Senia moved in with me this morning and I want Grandma to have a nice visit with us. Okay?'

She narrows her golden-brown eyes. 'In a mood? What does that even mean? You want me to pretend to be happy?'

As much as I want this meeting between Senia and Grandma to go smoothly, I can't tell her to pretend to be something she's not. 'No. I'm just asking you to remember that Senia picked you up when you were shitfaced and we never said a word about it to Grandma.' She casts her gaze downward at the grass and I glance over her shoulder at Grandma, who's waiting patiently in the car. I grab Molly's shoulder and plant a kiss on her forehead. 'It'll be okay, Moon. Come on.'

Grandma's leg bounces nervously the whole drive there, but the moment I pull into the semicircular driveway, she freezes. 'This is *yours*?'

I nod as I pull the car up next to the front steps. I want to say, *It can be yours, too.* I want to offer Grandma and Molly a place in my home, but I know Molly is dead set against changing schools and I don't want to cause her or Grandma any more stress.

Grandma's starry-eyed as I open the front door and she steps inside. 'This is *yours*?' she repeats the question and this gets a small chuckle out of Molly.

'Tristan, is that you?' Senia shouts from the kitchen. 'A delivery guy just came with—' Senia's surprised by us when she steps out of the kitchen. She glances at her T-shirt and short shorts and the embarrassment blooms in her cheeks. 'Why didn't you tell me you were bringing your family? Oh my God. I'm so embarrassed.'

'They delivered the pizza?' I ask her, but she's too busy being mortified.

I look at Grandma and she's smiling. 'I remember you,' she says to Senia. 'You're the one who got drunk at Molly's birthday party.'

Senia looks even more embarrassed now, if that's even possible. 'I'm so sorry. I had a drinking problem my freshman year. I'm so sorry.'

Grandma chuckles and waves away Senia's apology. 'Better to live life than watch from the sidelines.'

I've heard Grandma spout this droplet of wisdom plenty of times, but Senia looks surprised by the response. And even more surprised when Grandma Flo takes her into her arms. She wraps her arms around Grandma's shoulders and bites her lips as she instantly begins to tear up. She looks to me, her eyes pleading for some kind of guidance as to what she should do. All I do is nod and I think she knows what I mean: *Grandma knows about the baby.*

Grandma lets her go and her face scrunches up as she attempts to hold back her tears. 'Woo! I need a drink. Tristan, fix your grandma a whiskey sour, please.'

Senia gives Molly and Grandma a tour of the house while I fix her a drink and set out some plates for the pizza I had delivered. By the time they get back, Grandma has her arms hooked in Senia's and they're giggling like schoolgirls as they approach the dining table in the breakfast nook.

They all take their seats at the table and Grandma sits between Senia and me while Molly sits on my other side. Senia appears as if she's still on the verge of tears as she distributes slices of pizza to everyone. Finally, I grab Molly's hand and she glares at me.

'Moon, Senia and I are having a baby.'

She shakes her head and chuckles. 'What? Are you kidding me?'

'No,' I reply seriously and she turns to Senia.

Her eyes widen at the sincere look on Senia's face, then she yelps so loud I think I may need to get my hearing checked after this dinner. 'OMG!' she whispers. 'I'm gonna be an aunt.'

And once her tears begin, Senia and Grandma are free to join in. *Jesus Christ.* I'm going to have to escape all this estrogen soon or I may have to call up Chris and gab about my feelings for Senia.

Yeah, right.

An hour later, we've all gorged ourselves on pizza and baby talk. I offer Grandma and Molly the guest rooms to stay the night, but Grandma insists I take them home. I think she thinks she and Molly are intruding on my and Senia's alone time. She doesn't know that Senia and I have agreed to keep things friendly until we can figure out how we're going to raise this surprise baby.

After I drop them off and return home, I find Senia asleep on the sofa with the Science Channel playing on the TV. I turn off the TV and try not to grunt as I pick her up and carry her upstairs to her bed. I lay a soft kiss on her nose and quietly make my way out.

As I close the bedroom door behind me, I realize that I've changed. In the span of just a few weeks, I've gone from kicking girls out of my house to lovingly tucking them into the bed in my guest room. I sigh as I head for my bedroom with a pang of dark fear twisting inside my belly. Something bad is going to happen. I can feel it.

Chapter Nineteen

Our last five days of recording go smoothly. We wrap up the Friday before Christmas and return to my house to celebrate. I'm not surprised to find Senia and Claire already hanging out in the kitchen. As Chris, Claire, Jake, and Rachel discuss Jake and Rachel's wedding in the kitchen, I invite Senia into the living room to watch some TV. The Science Channel is showing a special on black holes and Senia quietly takes a seat next to me on the sofa to watch.

I'm not really watching the show. I keep stealing glances at the smooth skin on her legs and the way she subconsciously lays her hand protectively over her belly. I want to move her hand so I can place my hand there, but I'm pretty sure she's not far along enough for the baby to kick. But how awesome will it be to feel my little guy inside of her?

Once Jake and Rachel go through my last five beers as she attempts to beat him at a beer-guzzling contest, Chris and Claire offer to go and pick up some more.

'I've got more in the fridge in the guest house. Come on. I'll show you,' I say to Chris and he shrugs as he follows me outside.

I don't really need to show him where I keep the beer in the pool house and he knows that. I just need to talk to him.

After some small talk about whether our manager, Xander, is going to call us back to re-record something, I unlock the door to the guest house and turn on the lights. Chris heads straight for the refrigerator of the studio and I wait by the front door.

'I don't know what to get Senia for Christmas.'

Chris glances at me over his shoulder as he grabs two six-packs of Sam Adams out of the fridge. 'You haven't done that yet?'

'Hey, I'm not Mr Monogamy like you. I don't know how to do this shit.'

'So you're not fucking anyone else?' he asks as he makes his way out of the kitchenette.

He pushes a six-pack into my chest and I contemplate this question. I haven't fucked anyone since Chrissy on Thanksgiving. Well, unless you count the girl who worked at the grocery store that I hooked up with a few days ago, whatever her name was. She ran out to give me one of the bottles of Gatorade I dropped in the store and one thing led to another, but Senia and I haven't had sex since Yogurtland last month. It's a poor excuse for a terrible wrong, not at all made right by the fact that Senia and I aren't actually a couple yet, or the sickening regret that kept me awake that night.

Fuck. I'm such an asshole.

'No. I'm not fucking anyone else.' *From here on out.*

Chris looks skeptical as we make our way past the pool toward the patio. 'Then bare your fucking soul. Give her something that will only mean something to the two of you.'

'What the fuck does that mean?'

'You'll figure it out.'

Senia and I arrive at Grandma's house a little before noon on Christmas Day. Senia insists we need to arrive early so she can help Grandma cook. Since she had to lie to her family and say she was spending Christmas with Chris and Claire, I have to do as she says. Besides, it's kind of cool to watch her and Grandma laughing as they chop onions while I imagine the beat of my baby's heart as the background music.

When the food is simmering, Senia sends Grandma out of the kitchen to get some rest and calls me in to replace her. The sight of her in one of Grandma's aprons is weird, but strangely sexy.

'Can you set the table? We need plates and silverware, and bowls for the pumpkin soup.'

'Pumpkin soup?' I say, coming up behind her as she stirs the soup on the stove. She pushes my left hand away, but I reach forward and slide my right hand over her abdomen. 'You can't stand in my grandmother's kitchen, in that apron, barking orders at me, carrying my child, and not expect me to want to touch you. You can't expect me to not feel like I have some . . . claim on you.'

She lets out a deep sigh as I press my chest against her back. 'Tristan . . .' Her voice is breathy and full of longing. 'Please don't say stuff like that. It makes me want to either punch you or tear off your clothes. And I can't tell which one I want to do more.'

I slide my hand down and she freezes, but I quickly pull my hand back. 'I guess we'll find out soon.'

Grandma Flo makes us give thanks before we eat, the way she always does before every Christmas and Thanksgiving dinner, and Senia seems to be a pro at it.

'Thank you for the food and for inviting me into your home.' She turns to Molly and they both smile. 'Thank you for reminding me how much I never want to get drunk again. There are better ways to get wild. Trust me.' She winks at Molly and I shake my head. 'Thank you, Mrs Pollock, for giving me a place to celebrate Christmas – somewhere I can be myself.' Grandma smiles a crooked smile that seems to be masking whatever anguish, emotional or physical, she is feeling. 'Tristan,' Senia begins as she turns to me. She opens her mouth to say something, but nothing comes out.

'What?' I prompt her, but she closes her mouth and eyes and doesn't speak.

When she opens her eyes, I expect her to be crying. She seems to cry at the drop of a hat these days with all those hormones coursing through her. 'Excuse me,' she whispers as she rises from her chair and heads for the front door.

I follow after her and she stands on the porch steps where I just finished clearing the snow an hour ago, waiting for something. 'What's wrong?' She shakes her head and I step down onto the step below her so we're almost eye-level. 'Talk to me.'

'I've just never spent Christmas without my family.'

'I'll take you there. You don't have to stay here.'

'No, I have my car. If I wanted to leave, I'd go. You know that.'

'Is that why you brought your car?' I ask. 'I thought you brought it so you could stop by your parents' house and say hi to your family.'

'That is why I brought it . . . I . . .'

'I don't understand. If you want to be here, why are you upset?'

She steps sideways so our faces aren't so close and a thick cloud of steam escapes her mouth as she lets out a deep breath. 'It doesn't matter. I just need a minute. I'll come back inside soon.'

I wait a moment for her to change her mind and tell me she's coming inside, but she doesn't. 'It's cold. Don't stay out here too long.'

She closes her eyes and I take that as my cue to head back in. I leave the front door open and take a seat at the dining table, which, thankfully, still has a view of the front door.

'Where's Senia?' Molly asks as she sips a glass of cranberry juice.

'She's just missing her family a little. She'll be back inside in a couple of minutes.'

But a couple of minutes turns into nearly fifteen minutes and I have to check on her. When I open the door, Senia's car is gone. My first instinct is to hop into my car and go to her parents' house, but they don't know about me yet and I don't want to cause her any more trouble than she may already be in for not showing up to their Christmas dinner.

I pull my phone out of my pocket. It's a long-shot, but I have to at least try to call her. Not surprisingly, she doesn't answer, but I'm not upset because I've been a bit of an asshole to her about using her phone while driving. I look up and down the street, foolishly hoping she may have just parked a few houses away to think in the warmth of the car heater, but her car is nowhere. I wait a few minutes, to give her some time to get wherever she's going, then I begin typing a text message to her.

Me: *Where are you?*

I hesitate before I hit the send button. This text message sounds demanding. I swallow my pride and type two more words.

Me: *Where are you? I'm worried.*

I hit send and I get a response a few minutes later, just as Molly comes outside to see what's going on.

Senia: *I'm home. I'm in the study catching up on my homework.*

I'm confused. She just said that she was upset because she wasn't spending Christmas with her family and now she's gone home – to our home – instead of to her family's house. *Why do women have to be so fucking complicated?* I think as I reach into my pocket and grab my keys.

'Can I come with you?' Molly asks.

I smile. 'Not this time. I think Senia and I have some stuff to talk about.'

Molly laughs. 'You're whipped.'

'What? I am *not* whipped.'

'Yeah, you are. But that's okay. She's worth it.'

I shake my head as I head for my car. 'Tell Grandma she doesn't need to clean up. I'll send Lily over tomorrow morning.'

'Don't be a pussy!' she shouts at me as I slide into the driver's seat. 'Tell her how you feel.'

Chapter Twenty

Senia

I probably screwed things up with Tristan and his family, but I couldn't sit there and pretend like my mind wasn't elsewhere. And I couldn't tell Tristan what I was thinking. The last thing I need is for him to think I'm clingy and demanding. I needed a timeout.

So here I am in Tristan's study, which is right next door to the room where he practices bass for hours at a time. If he's that dedicated to his job, I should try to be that dedicated to my schoolwork. I can't let all this family stuff and all these emotions sidetrack me. But now that Tristan knows I'm here, I fully expect him to come walking through the door into the study and say something totally stupid or totally dreamy. It won't matter because, either way, it won't be the words I want to hear; the same words I nearly blurted out at his Grandma's dining table.

I'm such an idiot. I need to move out of here.

I grab my laptop and textbook then head back to my bedroom. I grab my suitcase out of the closet and begin stuffing the inner pocket with all my panties and bras. Then I pull a zipped case out from underneath the bed: my new goodie drawer since I know Tristan has probably searched all the drawers on this dresser.

'So that's where you keep it?'

His voice makes my skin ache. I want to turn around to face him, but I'm afraid of what his face will look like when he realizes I'm packing.

'Are you packing?'

I turn around and his eyes are narrowed, as if he's angry. 'I can't live here any more.'

'Is this because I asked you to have Christmas with us?'

'What? No! That's . . . that's not it at all. It's just . . .'

I try to think of a lie, but my mind is not working at normal speed. And the truth is not an option. I can't tell him I'm leaving because I'm in love with him. That just sounds stupid and if he doesn't feel the same . . . I don't know if I could handle finding out.

'What is it?' he asks as he takes a step toward me.

'I'm . . . I didn't get you anything for Christmas.'

He laughs as he reaches forward and grabs my hand. 'You're leaving because you didn't get me a present? Come on, what are you going to get me that I don't already have?'

Exactly what I thought when I was trying to figure

out what I was going to get him, which is why I had the brilliant idea of giving him . . . 'Me.'

His smile disappears and I know I've scared him. That's it. I have to leave. I shake his hand off and turn around to continue packing.

He grabs my elbow and turns me around, the muscle in his jaw twitching as his eyes search my face for something. 'I didn't get you anything either. Well, nothing you can unwrap and hold in your hands.' He takes a deep breath, steeling himself for whatever he's about to say. 'I know how much you hate commuting to class, so I rented an apartment near campus. I want us to move there before next semester.'

'An apartment?'

'Did you just say you're giving me *you* for Christmas?'

I think I'm going to be sick. Why did I say that? 'Sorry. It just sort of slipped out.'

I try to turn around again to continue packing, but he tightens his grip on my elbow. 'Look at me.' I look up into his fierce gray eyes and say a mental prayer that I don't vomit.

Chapter Twenty-One

This may be the biggest mistake of my life or the smartest thing I've ever done. All I know is that it has to be done. I can't watch her go so soon. Not on Christmas.

'When I asked Chris what I should get you, he told me I should get you something that means something only to me and you. I didn't know what the fuck that meant and I thought the apartment would be a great present, but I think you're better at this than I am. I need you to teach me. I need . . . I need you.' She bites her lip, but I can't tell if she's doing it to keep from crying or laughing. 'Say something.'

Finally, she smiles and I let out the breath I'm holding. 'I think what you mean is . . . I love you.'

My body tenses when I hear the words, but I know it's only because I haven't heard them in so long. 'You love me?'

She nods and a strange sensation builds inside me that is so powerful it lights the hollow of my chest on fire. *Is this what love feels like? 'Cause it fucking hurts.*

I grab the sides of her head and tilt her face up. There's a weird trembling in my chest, but my hands are steady and firm as I look her in the eye. 'I love you. Nothing else can explain how crazy you make me. And I want you to stay with me, tonight, tomorrow, and . . . for as long as it takes to make this right, because I know everything seems completely fucked up right now. But it won't always be that way. We'll get it right, won't we?'

She nods again and a tear rolls down her cheek. 'We'll get it right,' she whispers. 'Eventually.'

I smile as I lean in to kiss her cheek and the taste of her tears is better than I remember it. I kiss the corner of her mouth and her hands glide up to grab handfuls of my hair. She kisses me hard as I slide my hands under her UNC T-shirt. Her skin is so warm and soft. I can only imagine how much softer it will get over the next few months.

I yank my hoodie off then I pull her shirt over her head. She drags out the moment, moving at an achingly slow pace as she unclasps her lacy white bra and lets it fall to the floor. Her nipples are stiff and inviting. She moans into my mouth as I kiss her and press my chest against hers.

'Are you ready to be fucked?' I whisper as I move down to kiss her neck.

She throws her head back and lets out a throaty laugh that's sexy as hell. 'Oh, Tristan.'

'What?'

She smiles as she traces her finger along my jawline, then she looks me in the eye. 'Are you ready to have your world turned inside out?'

I let out a soft chuckle and her smile turns me on even more. 'Baby, you can turn me inside out, upside down, sideways . . . whatever position you prefer. I'm ready when you are.'

'I have more than a few positions in mind.'

She reaches for my waistband, but she doesn't unbutton my jeans. She grabs my waistband and attempts to push me toward the bed, but I'm too solid to be moved.

She laughs sheepishly and I kiss her forehead. 'You can always just ask and I'd be happy to lie down for you.'

'Can you please lie down?'

'No. You lie down.'

'Are we going to argue about this?'

'Nope, because you're going to do exactly as I say and you're not going to argue with me. Now strip down and lie on the bed.'

I shove her suitcase off the bed as she undresses, then I unzip her goodie bag. Sifting through the contents, I find an assortment of tools, most of which I've used before, but some are a bit foreign, and that intrigues me. First things first, I undress and slip a soft rubber cock ring down to the base of my erection; there will be no premature ejaculation tonight. I glance over at

Senia and she's biting her lip as she watches me. I pull out a smooth pink vibrator that's as big as my dick, then I lie down next to her. She reaches for me, but I push her hands away.

'You're not allowed to touch me. Just close your eyes and try not to scream too loud.'

She giggles nervously as she closes her eyes and I turn the vibrator on. I press it against the crook of her neck then I slowly trace a line over the hollow of her throat and down to her chest. She's breathing faster now and I'm getting harder just watching her chest move quickly up and down. I lightly brush the vibrator over her nipple and she squeezes her eyes tightly shut as she whispers, 'Oh, God.'

I trace a light circle around her areola with the vibrator, then I take her nipple into my mouth. I alternate between sucking and flicking and her back begins to arch.

'Try not to move.'

She lets out a nervous chuckle. 'Impossible.'

I trail the vibrator over her other nipple then I run it down over her abdomen. I plant a soft kiss just below her navel and I can feel her muscles tense with anticipation.

'Just breathe,' I murmur as I slide the vibrator over her mound and stop there. 'Relax.'

I gently spread her legs open and position myself between them. The perfect landing strip of hair I remember from the last time we did this a month ago has grown out a little. I trace the vibrator gently over her slit and she gasps. I keep going until I reach her cheeks then I move back up. I do this a few more times until she's glistening wet, then I slide the vibrator inside of her, just a few inches, and immediately cover her clit with my mouth.

'Jesus fucking Christ!' she cries, as I angle the vibrator upwards and suck lightly.

'That's not my name,' I say, then I swirl my tongue and gently press my forearm down on her abdomen to hold her steady as her hips begin to buck.

'Tristan,' she breathes as her body quivers beneath me. 'Oh, God, Tristan.'

She grabs my hair and lets out a blood-curdling scream as I finish her off. She begins to pull me up by my hair, but I push her hands away. I turn off the vibrator and set it aside as I continue to stimulate her with my mouth. But this time I slide a finger between her cheeks and her entire body contracts around me as I give her another earth-shattering orgasm.

'Oh my God,' she whispers repeatedly as I kiss my way up her belly.

She's limp as a wet rag as I slide my arm beneath her lower back and lift her slightly so I can slide into her. She winces as I hit her cervix and the cock ring hits her sensitive clit. She wraps her arms around my shoulders and I tilt my head back to look at her. We lock eyes and I suddenly feel as if I'm right where I'm supposed to be.

Thrusting into her slowly, I lean my forehead against hers and she tightens her arms around my shoulders. We play like this, a sort of back-and-forth game of giving and receiving; completely lost in each other for hours. I don't notice the four missed calls or the three voicemail messages flashing on my phone until the next morning – until it's too late.

Chapter Twenty-Two

Poetry is defined as a literary work in which special intensity is given to the expression of feelings and ideas by the use of distinctive style and rhythm. This is also what music does. I've never considered myself a poet. And the fact that I haven't written a song in more than three years makes me even less worthy of this title. But waking up next to Senia in the guest bedroom sparks a flash of inspiration and I think of two lines:

The day our wires crossed,
You were broken, I was lost.

I'm sure the logical conclusion would be that now, somehow, Senia is whole and I am found. The truth is love isn't like that. I think I'm finally starting to realize that love isn't about fixing things or people. It's about sticking around when things can't be fixed.

I slide out of Senia's bed, smiling as I think of how tonight this bed will be put out of commission as she joins me in the master bedroom. I quietly pull on some boxers then head downstairs to make the usual fried egg and toast I see her making for herself in the morning. When I get downstairs, I find my phone on the kitchen island. I try to check the notifications, but it's dead. It always happens when I forget to leave it charging at night. Who fucking cares? I fucked like a champ last night.

I fix Senia's breakfast – tripling the quantities so I can have some and in case she wants extra – then I carry it all upstairs on a tray my interior decorator left on the coffee table a few months ago. When I enter the guest room, the sight of her hugging her pillow and smiling takes my breath away.

'I made you the usual,' I say, taking a cue from Chris and Claire and how well they know each other's breakfast choices. She scoots back so I can set the tray on the bed next to her. 'I'll be right back. I have to put my phone charging.'

I hook the phone up to the charger in the study then I head back to the guest room. Senia is sitting up, cross-legged, on the bed with a piece of toast in her hand, grinning. This domestic stuff isn't so hard.

I sit down next to her and plop a fried egg onto a piece of toast then chow down. 'What are your plans today?' I ask through a mouthful of food.

She reaches up and wipes something from the corner of my mouth before she answers. 'I have to read this physics paper so I can have my response ready when classes start in a few weeks. I hate physics.'

I pour us both a glass of orange juice from the pitcher and take a sip before I respond. 'I don't know shit about physics, but I can help you if you need something else done.'

She chuckles. 'Are you gonna wash my laundry?'

I roll my eyes as I place the glass of juice down. 'That's what I'm supposed to do, I guess. I'm done recording but you're still studying. I have to be the one to step up, right? Give me your stinky laundry and I'll throw it in the laundry room. I'm sure Lily will do a great job washing it tomorrow.'

'You're such an asshole.'

'That's why you love me.'

Her smile disappears as she brings the glass of orange juice to her lips. 'That really happened, didn't it?'

She's referring to the fact that we both said those three words last night, so I nod. 'Yeah, pretty crazy, I'd say, considering both of our track records.'

'Well, I think I've confessed my love for every guy I've dated since freshman year, but don't let that make you self-conscious. Last night was . . . different.'

'Different?' I say, because I'm not quite sure how to respond to the fact that she's used those three words so casually in the past.

'Well, first of all, I don't think I've ever had three orgasms in the span of ten minutes.'

'I was just easing you in. Next time will be better.'

She shakes her head as she dips her toast in the

runny egg yolk. 'That. That's what's different. You always call me out on my shit.' She takes a bite of toast and I reach across to wipe some of the yolk from the corner of her mouth. 'I thought I was going to show you some tricks last night, but I guess it's hard to teach an old dog new tricks.'

The word 'tricks' triggers a deep nausea in the pit of my stomach and I have to swallow my vomit. I set down the piece of toast I just picked up and stand from the bed. 'Be back as soon as I can.'

I set off to the study to clear my head and check my phone. When I see I have a missed call and a message from Lily and four missed calls from Grandma Flo, I panic a little. I call her right back without bothering to check the voicemail messages.

'Oh my goodness, I've been trying to call you all morning,' she declares when she answers the phone. 'And I tried calling you last night about the presents you left. Did you get my messages?'

'I didn't listen to them yet. What's so urgent? I can pick the presents up another time.'

'Oh, my,' she whispers. 'Oh, no, no, no. I'm so sorry, honey. I didn't mean to, but Lily came over this morning and when she called you to tell you she won't be coming in tomorrow, I saw your address on her phone. I asked if I could copy it down. I just thought maybe I could send you and Senia's gifts to your house since you both left in a hurry. I didn't want you to have to make another trip back here.'

I don't have to listen to any more to know why she's apologizing for taking down my address. 'Where's Elaine?'

'She's on her way.'

The dead silence that follows this sentence is filled with all the things I've never told anyone. All the tiny lies I've told myself over the years about how none of it matters. It was a moment in time that can be forgotten – maybe even erased. I'm nobody special and the things that happened to me a million years ago affect no one, just me.

But it keeps getting more and more difficult to believe that when I see the fallout. The broken trust I'd begun to repair with Grandma and Molly when I invited them over last weekend is nothing but dust now, settling over the wreckage of my past. And it's not their fault. It's my fault for believing I could just walk around the wreckage. Pretend it isn't there. Pretend it doesn't matter.

It so obviously matters. Nothing has ever mattered more.

Chapter Twenty-Three

Nine Years Ago

This is the last time. I know she said that about the last two times, but this time I'm not backing down. If I have to do this again after today, I'll know that she's full of shit – as I suspected.

I enter the dingy bedroom at the back of the house, where the sweet smell of crack-pipe always lingers. My gaze immediately darts to the corner of the room, where the john usually sits in the cruddy armchair next to a small table stocked with all the essentials: tissues, lube, condoms, and other shit I'd never seen or heard of until three weeks ago. When I see the person sitting in the chair, I'm dumbstruck. It's a woman.

It's usually some fat, mangy, perverted asshole who wants to get off to two kids getting it on. This woman is not fat or mangy. She looks like a fucking school-teacher with her coral-pink sweater and gray slacks.

She's careful not to touch the arms of the chair as she sits with one leg draped over the other and her hands clasped over her knee.

Elaine's voice startles me out of my stupor and I turn toward the bed. The girl lying on the bed looks young, maybe even younger than me. Her brown hair has been styled in pigtails, her round brown eyes are wide with fear, and she's wearing nothing but a bra and a schoolgirl skirt.

Vomit stings the back of my throat and, before I can stop it, a small stream of partially digested toast oozes out of my mouth. I catch it with my hand and Elaine sighs. 'That's disgusting. Go wash your hands.'

I glance at the girl as I leave the bedroom and her eyes are closed as tears stream down her face. I race to the bathroom and lock the door behind me. I dump the vomit out of my hand and into the sink, then I reach for the faucet to wash my hands. The faucet handle is splattered with blood, as is the countertop and the wall behind the sink. The blood is fresh, too. Someone must have just shot up in here.

Grabbing a wad of toilet paper, I use it as a shield between my hand and the faucet handle as I turn the water on. I wash my hands in super-hot water and lots of soap then I take a seat on the toilet.

I should just leave. Even if this is the last time I have to do this, it's not worth it. The girl's face, her tears, flash in my mind and I try not to think the obvious. If

I don't do it to her, they'll get somebody else – someone who may hurt her.

I hate it here.

I hate it here.

I hate it here.

I drag myself out of the bathroom and trudge back down the hallway toward the sweet, acrid stench of hopelessness. When I enter the bedroom, the girl is sitting cross-legged on the bed, holding her skirt down between her legs to cover herself up.

'Tristan, this is Ashley,' Elaine declares. Then she whispers in my ear, 'This is the last one. I promise.'

Chapter Twenty-Four

I try to temper my anger as I make my way back to the guest room. When I enter, I nearly bump into Senia as she walks out of the room with the breakfast tray.

'I'll take that,' I say, taking the tray from her hands. 'You go take a shower. I have to run to the store real quick to grab a Christmas card for Lily. Do you need anything?'

She looks confused by my plans. 'Christmas was yesterday. And I already gave Lily a card with her bonus on Christmas Eve. I told you.'

'Oh, yeah. I guess I forgot.' I try to quickly come up with another reason to leave, but I'm so anxious I can't think straight. 'I have to go pick up our presents from Grandma's house. She just called to ask if she could send them, but I told her I'd go pick them up.'

When lying, it's always best to go with an explanation that closely resembles the truth.

She still looks perplexed; probably wondering why I need to get the presents now rather than later. But she relents and proceeds to gather some fresh clothes so she can take a shower. When she reaches into her suitcase for some panties, I snatch them out of her hand and toss them into the corner.

'You won't be needing those.' She grins as I kiss her cheekbone. 'I'll be right back.'

I race downstairs and jump in my car, then I drive down to the entrance of Giovanni Court and park. I forgot to ask Grandma if Elaine was coming alone, so I have my Glock 23 on the seat next to me. The last thing I need is to get into it with one of her strung-out boyfriends. I wait exactly twelve minutes before I see the front of her maroon minivan coming down Venetian. I pull my car around the corner and flip a hard left in front of her so she has to slam on her brakes. I stuff the gun into the back of my waistband then I hop out of the car and head straight for the driver's side of the minivan. I wrench the door open and her eyes are wide, but there's a shocked smile on her face.

'Get out!' I order her and she fumbles a little with the seatbelt before she slides out of the van.

I immediately begin searching her car and quickly find her cell phone and the small Post-it note where my address is scrawled in Grandma's shaky handwriting. I drop the paper on the asphalt and smash it with my sneaker until it's disintegrated. Then I search for my contact information in her phone and, sure enough, she already entered it in there. She laughs as I delete my address and phone number from her phone and search all her notes apps and social apps to make sure she didn't save it somewhere else.

'Don't you ever fucking come here again,' I growl as I throw her phone into the interior of her car. 'This is your first and only warning: forget my address.'

She's still smiling as she reaches into the van toward the front seat. I slide my hand behind my back and prepare for the worst. But she doesn't pull out a gun.

'Petition for full custody of Molly,' she says, handing me a large white envelope. 'I already gave your grandma a copy. I came all the way out here, out of the kindness of my heart, to give you one.'

I snatch the envelope out of her hand and glance at the return address: Debra Holstein, Esq.

'You're fucking deluded if you think I'd ever let that happen. But that's why you're here, isn't it? You think you've got me where you want me because you know where I live. You think I'm scared you're going to send your crackhead boyfriends or some fucking reporters over here. Well, you're wrong. Because I don't live here any more. Now get the fuck out of here before I call Debra Holstein and tell her everything.'

Her smile finally fades and she slowly gets back into the car. 'This isn't over. Someone gets Grandma's house when she dies and you sure as hell don't need it,' she says, glancing around at the sprawling properties on Venetian Court. 'You've always been so selfish.'

She slams the door shut and it takes everything in me not to pull the gun out of my waistband and shoot.

I don't know what I'd shoot. Maybe just shooting her tires would make me feel better. But I'm too fucking chickenshit to find out.

I watch as she drives away, waiting a few minutes after her car is out of sight before I drive back to the house. This time I put my car in the garage and I head back inside. I lock up the gun and stuff the envelope behind some books in the study, then I go upstairs. Senia is lying on my bed on her stomach with her laptop in front of her.

I panicked a little when I saw her lying on the floor in the study the other day. I was worried that maybe lying on her stomach would squish the baby. It sent her into a crying fit, so I decided I wouldn't make any more comments about what's best for the baby. She's going to her first doctor's appointment after we get back from Jake and Rachel's wedding in Vegas next week. She'll only be about seven weeks along by then. Everything will be fine.

She's wearing a tank top and panties and just the sight of her calms me. She doesn't know anything about Elaine or the shit I've done, but I think Senia's the kind of person who might understand . . . in a few years when I've trapped her.

'You're back early. Where are the gifts?' she asks as she watches me approach the bed.

'I decided not to go. I forgot to plug in the car last night.'

'You and your damn electric car.'

'I did take a few minutes to look around the garage for those old pictures of Molly you wanted for the photo book. Couldn't find them, but I'll keep looking. And, hey, that car you gave Claire a couple of months ago was a hybrid. But I don't do hybrid. I go all the way.'

She shakes her head as I take a seat on the bed and slide my hand under her shirt to feel the smooth skin on her back. 'What are you grinning at?' she asks breathlessly.

'Just thinking that I have *a lot* of plans for you.'

She closes her eyes as I lightly brush my fingertips over her skin. 'Plans? When exactly are we moving into this apartment you got?'

'It will be ready after the fifteenth of January. I'm having them make a few changes.'

'What kind of changes?'

I slip my hand out of her shirt and brush her hair aside so I can kiss the back of her neck. 'They're turning the shower into a steam shower.'

She laughs and the vibration of her laughter against my lips gets me hot. 'I am *not* having sex with you in a steam room!'

'It's not a steam room. It's a steam *shower*.'

'Same difference.'

I grab her hips and flip her over onto her back. She grins at me as I close her laptop and set it on the floor. 'You have three weeks to write that paper. But you have about three seconds before I throw that fucking computer in the fireplace.'

I slide my hand into her panties and she squirms as I lightly caress her clit. I lean in to kiss her and she grabs my shoulders to stop me.

'Wait. It's your turn today.'

She instructs me to sit on the edge of the bed as she kneels before me and gives me what can only be described as the best fucking blowjob I've ever received.

What follows is an act, but I've become a great actor. I can pretend to be somewhere I'm not. I can pretend to be someone I'm not. And right now, I'm pretending to be someone whose life isn't crumbling on all sides of them.

Chapter Twenty-Five

'You have to meet my parents today,' Senia blurts out as we walk through the parking lot toward the bridal shop to pick up her dress for the double wedding in Vegas. I'm careful to hold her arm in case we hit a patch of ice. The snow that came three days ago on Christmas Day is mostly melted, but it's still cold as hell out here. And I've slipped on enough invisible ice in my lifetime to know better. The last thing I need right now is for something to happen to Senia or the baby.

'Today? Isn't that kind of soon?'

The words come out before I can even stop myself. I open the door to the shop and she enters ahead of me, but she doesn't answer my question as she proceeds to examine the dress the woman behind the counter hands to her. I try not to look bored or really fucking uncomfortable as they stand there talking about flowers and wedding cakes. They're both gushing over the surprise wedding that Chris planned for Claire and how romantic it is. I'm trying really hard not to roll my eyes.

'Oh, I'm sorry. Is it too soon for you to be hearing this conversation?' Senia asks, her head tilted to one side, probably because it's weighed down by all that sarcasm.

I grin as I look her in the eye without flinching. 'Maybe, but I doubt that'll stop you.'

She glares at me then says goodbye to the shop owner. I lock my arm in hers again as we make it out to the parking lot and she tries to wrench her arm free, but I just tighten my hold on her.

'How do you go from being practically perfect to complete asshole in less than two seconds?'

'It's a talent I've perfected and you should probably get used to it.'

She tries to free her arm again, this time pushing me away with one hand while she pulls the other arm free. 'Don't touch me.'

I allow her to walk by herself and everything is fine until she steps over a parking bumper and slips on some melted snow. She curses spectacularly as her ass hits the concrete bumper. Rushing to her side to help her, I have to step back to dodge her open hand as she attempts to slap me.

'Get away from me!'

'Are you okay?'

I offer my hand to help her up, but she stands easily on her own. 'My ass hurts. And it's *your* fault!'

I try not to laugh at this. She was complaining this morning about her ass hurting. I warned her before I took her from behind last night, but she insisted she could handle it.

I open the car door for her and she gets inside without further insult. Rounding the front of the car, I get inside quickly so I can crank up the heater. She pulls off her gloves and tucks them between her legs. When she looks up at me, the anger is gone.

'Do you really think it's too soon for you to meet my parents?'

'No, it's not. That was just an automatic response. I'm . . . sorry. I want to meet your folks.'

'You *want* to meet them?'

'Okay, maybe not yet, but I'm sure the nerves will subside. But . . . you should know that parents usually hate me. There's just something about me.'

I try not to smile as I think of all the dicks I've had to deal with over the years: brothers and friends of girls I've dated who thought they could talk enough crap about me to change those girls' minds. You can't force someone to see that something is bad for them. You just have to sit back and watch people reach for the flame – sometimes repeatedly – until they finally understand that fire hurts.

'Yeah, there is something about you. It's your asshole-y-ness.'

'His Asshole-y-ness. I suppose I deserve that title.'

She shakes her head as I pull the car out of the parking space. 'My parents want to take you to a Salvadoran restaurant.'

'I like burritos.'

'You have so much to learn. Just let me do most of the talking. We're not there to tell them about the baby. They just want to meet you before we go to Vegas. They still don't know we're living together.'

I pull onto the highway to head toward her parents' neighborhood and I begin to feel an itch in the pit of my stomach, a restlessness that makes me want to turn the car around and forget all of it.

Suddenly, I'm reminded of the first time I met Ashley's adoptive parents. They had taken her in as a foster child shortly after her appearances at Elaine's house. She was completely broken and she even turned to drugs for a while, but they cleaned her up, adopted her, put her in a different school to get her away from her old friends, and she was able to pretend to be okay – until we ended up in the same art class.

Chris had quit school the summer before our junior year, so it was just Jake and me left at Athens Drive High School. Jake was a senior, so the only classes we ever shared at ADHS were elective classes. We didn't get placed in any of the same electives during my junior year. But I recognized Ashley the moment I saw her sitting in the back of the class with her brown hair looking a bit disheveled and hardly any make-up, unlike the last time I saw her in that back bedroom with her black mascara streaming down her cheeks.

'You missed the exit,' Senia says. 'Are you okay?'

'Just thinking about Molly.'

I want to tell her everything. I do. But the shame and disgust I feel for the things I did to Ashley nine years ago couldn't be erased by years of perspective or thirteen months of her trying to prove that she did forgive me. I knew when she cheated on me that she did it to make it easier for her to go to college and leave me behind – to leave everything that happened between us behind. But you can't leave behind the kind of demons that cling to your back, leaving you weighed down and misshapen.

Ashley's friend, Beatrice, left me a voicemail message last year to tell me that Ashley had just come back from a fashion internship in Paris. For a few days, I considered returning her call, just to know why Ashley wanted me to know this. Then it dawned on me that she wanted me to know that she's doing well. She had to get away from me to be okay.

'I think Molly should move in with us,' Senia says as I take the next exit.

'She doesn't want to change schools. She doesn't want to lose her friends.' *And I don't blame her.*

After Chris dropped out and Jake and Ashley graduated, that's where the endless stream of meaningless sex and relationships began for me. I don't want Molly to go looking for something to fill the void once her grandmother and her friends are taken from her.

'But Chapel Hill is just forty minutes from her school. I've been driving forty minutes to get to school every day,' Senia continues. 'And I'm sure Jackie would let her use her address so it looks like she still resides within the district lines.'

I'm positive Chris's mom, Jackie, would allow Molly to use her address, but that's not what I'm most worried about.

'What about Grandma? I can't leave her alone in that house.'

'She could come too,' she replies without hesitation. 'She could have our bedroom and we'll sleep on a sofa bed or something. It will be . . . *comfortable*.'

'You have a warped idea of what constitutes *comfortable* living conditions.'

She shrugs as I turn onto the main road. 'Whatever. I just think it would be good for Molly.'

And that itchy restlessness in the pit of my stomach is gone. I reach for her hand and she smiles as I give it a gentle squeeze. Maybe Senia understands more than I give her credit for.

The day our wires crossed,
You were broken, I was lost.
But I found my way to you,
To a place I didn't know was true.
Now I can't conceive of living without the sound of us too.

Chapter Twenty-Six

We're nearly at the restaurant when Senia's phone rings. It's her parents informing her that the restaurant reservation has been canceled. Dinner will take place at her parents' house. I turn the car around – again – and ten minutes later we arrive at a large two-story stucco house in a country-club housing tract in North Raleigh.

I know Senia's family does well with the family real estate business, but I did sort of fantasize that her family's house would be a rundown shack I rescued her from. I reach for the door handle to exit the car, but Senia grabs my arm.

'Wait!' She holds my face and kisses me hard – the kind of kiss that melts your insides and makes you want to stay under the covers all day. 'Just wanted to get it out of the way since I won't be able to do that for a while.'

I chuckle as she lets go of my face and hops out of the car. We walk hand-in-hand toward the front door, passing under a bare bougainvillea archway that drips with melting snow. I'm not sure what she's thinking, but I'm thinking that this feels an awful lot like walking down the aisle. She reaches for the doorknob and, I swear, the next twenty minutes are a slow-motion blur of handshakes and hugs. I can't really remember much of it, but I do remember someone grabbing my ass and the look on Senia's father's face when he sees me.

He's wearing a gray suit and he's in good shape for a man his age. His dark hair is cropped short and impeccably styled. I can't tell if he looks more like a real estate agent or a mobster. His nostrils flare as his gaze takes in my shoulder-length hair, my gray jeans and the black sweater I'm wearing under my army-green twill jacket.

I hold my hand out to him. 'Nice to meet you, sir.'

He cocks an eyebrow, exactly the way Senia does when she's not impressed. 'Aren't you going to remove your jacket?' he says with a slight accent that makes me feel as if I've stepped into a scene from the movie *Scarface*. I begin to take my jacket off and he laughs. 'I'm only kidding!' He holds his hand out for me to shake. When I take it, he pulls me into a bone-crushing hug, which gives him the perfect opportunity to whisper in my ear: 'Keep it in your pants in Las Vegas, okay?'

I swallow hard as he lets me go and he's still wearing a huge smile. He nods and I nod just enough for him to notice, then I try not to smile. We'll only be in Vegas for two nights. I can handle two nights without sex. Good thing is, with Senia being pregnant, I don't have to.

Dinner actually goes pretty well after that. Senia's mom serves up some fried fish and something called *pupusas*, which just look like fat tortillas stuffed with cheese and various meats. Senia rolls her eyes when I tell her I hope this food doesn't give me explosive *pupusa*, then her cheeks flush red when I ask her for some ketchup for my fried fish. Just the sight of me pouring the ketchup onto my plate makes her mom, Nancy, cringe. Fried food always tastes better with ketchup. They'll learn.

Senia's three older sisters are a whole different story. They ogle me all through dinner and I catch Senia burning them with her laser eyes multiple times. None of them are as hot as Senia, but her sister Maribel, who's just two years older than Senia, keeps glancing at me as she blathers on about her volunteer work at the local boys' and girls' club. It starts to make me a little uncomfortable, so I reach up and pretend to wipe something from the corner of Senia's mouth.

'What is it?' Senia asks as she attempts to wipe her face clean.

'Nothing. Just a piece of *pupu . . . sa*. I got it.'

'You think that's funny?'

'I think you're smiling.'

I kiss her cheek and she pushes me away gently. 'Stop.'

But Senia's little sister Sophie, who Senia proudly

claims to have named, is the most persistent of them all. She sits next to me on the couch as the family watches football and we draw pictures. She draws pictures of all the new friends she's made in kindergarten and I draw a picture of Molly. She trades drawings with me and asks me to draw something on her picture. I think this is her subtle way of trying to get me to improve her drawing. So I add a sketch of Senia and me on the right side of the page and she makes me squeeze in a picture of her so the three of us are together.

Senia pretends to be playing on her phone the whole time, but I catch her stealing glances at Sophie and me every once in a while with a tiny smile curling the corners of her lips. By the time we leave her parents' house, I'm confident I passed the test, if only for the blood-curdling tantrum that Sophie threw when I told her it was time for me to leave. After I've pulled my car into the garage and plugged it in to charge overnight, Senia and I take my tuxedo and her maid-of-honor dress upstairs and go straight to bed.

I don't know if this is what it feels like to be in an adult relationship, but if it is, then I could get used to it. It feels good to be adored. But knowing that there's only one girl who *I* adore is freeing. Unless the little sac of DNA inside Senia's belly is a girl. Then I'll have two girls to adore. In which case, the more the better.

Chapter Twenty-Seven

I don't know what I'm more nervous about today: being the best man in both my best friends' weddings or the fact that Senia's parents found out about the baby yesterday.

Senia wasn't feeling well yesterday, so I took a trip to the grocery store to replenish her supply of saltine crackers. I didn't know that her oldest sister Claudia had come over to visit while I was gone. If I'd known, I wouldn't have called out *How's my incubator?* while approaching the bedroom. Between the incubator comment and the saltine crackers, it didn't take long for Claudia to figure out our secret.

I'm trying not to panic now that the pregnancy is out in the open, but I have a million questions racing through my mind. Will her father insist we get married? And what about the tour this summer? Will I have to cancel? What will Chris think? I can't leave Senia here while she's eight months pregnant.

I wish Grandma and Molly could be here to see

the wedding. They both love Chris and Claire, but Grandma's in too much pain. I don't want to think of the possibility that she may not make it to September, when the baby's due.

I leave Senia with Claire so they can get ready for the wedding, then Chris, Jake, and I head out of the hotel to a tattoo shop in downtown Vegas.

'So you're still not going to tell us what you're getting?' Jake says with a laugh when I refuse for the twentieth time to tell him and Chris what I'm getting tattooed on my wrist today. 'That's weak.'

'That's weak?' I reply incredulously. 'I'm not the one getting Jay-Rae and today's date tattooed on my wrist. That's some weak shit right there.'

Chris and Jake are both getting their wedding dates tattooed on their wrists, but I'm not getting married tonight. I racked my brain trying to come up with something I could get tattooed on the inside of my wrist that was both small enough and significant enough to display so prominently. What I decided on was something that makes sense to me and only me. Maybe someday, it will make sense to the person I allow into my fucked-up world forever.

After we leave the shop with our tattoos conveniently covered in gauze, I get a text from Senia telling me to meet her in tent number six. The wedding is being held in the middle of the desert with Jake and Rachel saying their vows at 11.30 p.m. and Chris and Claire saying their vows at midnight. Chris insisted on paying for the entire wedding so that he would have the privilege of getting married as the clock strikes twelve. If I had half as much money as that asshole does, I'd probably do the same.

When the band broke up briefly last year, while Chris was recording in L.A., Jake and I used to get drunk and try to figure out the terms of Chris's recording contract. It turns out our guesses were way off the mark, but I'm not complaining. Even if Chris does earn about seven times as much as Jake and me, I'm happy with the fuck-ton of money I made this year. And to show Chris that there are no hard feelings, I got him a wedding present that he will never forget and that I guarantee will top every other gift he and Claire receive today.

After I shower and change into my tux, I hop in a cab and head for the desert. It's about 9.30 p.m. when the cab pulls into the sandy lot. The half-dozen tents they have set up for the wedding glow like paper lanterns on a blanket of sand. They've laid paths of grass and lights between the tents so no one gets lost. It's freezing out here. I hope Senia's wearing something that will keep her warm.

I can't knock on the silk tent, but I can see silhouettes moving inside. 'Knock-knock,' I call out and the sounds of shuffling come as a reply.

Senia appears at the entrance to the tent, still wearing a T-shirt and sweat pants and rollers in her hair. She takes one look at me in my tux and her jaw goes slack. 'That is so fucking hot.'

'You're not so bad yourself. The curlers really work with that ensemble.'

'Shut up. I can't get dressed until all my make-up is done. I paid six hundred dollars for that dress. I can't get make-up on it.'

'Why did you pay for the dress? I would have paid for it.'

'Uh, hello? You were standing right there when I forked over my credit card the other day at the bridal shop and you never said anything about paying. You were probably too busy trying to block out our conversation.'

'Sorry. I guess I *was* trying to tune it out.'

She reaches up and adjusts my hair a little. 'Do you mind if I fix your hair later? I have to finish Rachel right now.'

I laugh at this suggestion. 'Yes, I do mind. Is that why you asked me to come here?' She smiles sheepishly as she reaches for my hair again and I push her hand away. 'You're not doing anything to this hair. I'm like Samson: my hair is my strength. No one touches this hair except my hairdresser Kali. Understood?'

'Ooh, you *do* take your hair seriously. I *like* that.' She plants a soft kiss on my lips then turns around to head back into the tent. 'Jake is in tent number five. See you in a couple of hours, best man.'

Jake and I hang out in tent number five for a while, taking shots of tequila as we wait for Chris to arrive. Chris isn't a big drinker when he's with Claire, but I can always count on Jake to get plastered with me. And I'm really fucking nervous right now. Not about the weddings; about the toast and the wedding gift, and I'm nervous about Senia seeing this tattoo.

By our fourth shot of tequila, Jake's reddish-brown hair and beard are starting to look a little disheveled. 'Maybe you should slow down,' I suggest. I grab the bottle of tequila off the glass tabletop before he can pour another shot. 'You don't want to forget your vows.'

'I can't believe I'm getting married to Rachel,' he slurs.

I try not to laugh at this declaration. Rachel has always been a supreme bitch – always saying what's on her mind with no regard for anyone's feelings. She has absolutely no filter between her brain and her mouth. But despite that, I think Jake is lucky to have her. She's dug him out of so many holes over the years. She even drove his mom to all her radiation appointments when she got skin cancer on her arm last year.

'You can't believe you're getting married? Or you can't believe it's Rachel you're marrying?'

'I can't believe she wants to marry me.'

'What the fuck are you talking about? You're Jay-Rae! You're gonna get your matching Jay-Rae pillow-cases and she'll give birth to two-point-five beards. And Jay-Rae will live happily ever after.'

He smiles reluctantly. 'Show me that fucking tattoo.'

The tequila swirls in my belly at the sound of these words. I consider blowing him off, then I realize that there is absolutely no way he'll know what it means. I pull the gauze and tape off my wrist and hold it up for him to see.

He leans forward in his chair and squints. 'One, two, three. What does that mean?'

'Nothing important,' I reply, standing from the chair and taking the bottle of tequila with me toward the vanity area. I put the bottle down on the surface of the white vanity and proceed to cover the tattoo again. 'Come on. You have to drink some water and try to sober up a little. You're on in forty minutes.'

Once Jake and Rachel say their vows, I set off to find Chris to give him his wedding gift before his ceremony begins. I stop him just as he's heading for the big tent.

'What's up?' Chris asks as he tucks his phone into his pocket.

I feel nervous; like, so nervous I'm almost sick to my stomach. Why the fuck am I so nervous about giving my best friend his wedding present? Maybe it has to do with the sheer magnitude of the gift.

'I want to give you and Claire your wedding gift before everything gets crazy. Do you mind? It's in there,' I say, nodding toward the tent where Jake and I were downing tequila shots earlier.

'You just can't wait until later to give me that blowjob, can you?'

I shrug as we head for the tent. 'Nah, that can wait until later. And this present is much better since I'm not nearly as good at sucking dick as you are.'

We enter the tent and I immediately head for the purple bag where Senia packed the present with her gazillion styling tools. That girl and her obsession with hair and make-up are going to make me go broke. I pull a thick, white envelope out of the bag and hand it to Chris.

Chris stares at it for a moment, trying to figure it out. 'What the fuck is this?'

'It's the deed to my house. I don't want it any more. Senia and I are moving to Chapel Hill so she doesn't have to commute to school next semester.'

'Are you fucking kidding me? I don't want your house.'

He tries to push the envelope into my hand, but I take a step back and shake my head. 'It's done. I already gifted it to you. I already put a deposit on an apartment off campus. The house is yours.' He runs his fingers through his hair as he stares at the envelope in my hand. 'I know you and Claire wanted a house with a good piece of land.'

He shakes his head in disbelief, but soon a smile comes over his face and his eyes light up as if he has an idea. 'You can have my condo. There's still eleven months on the lease.'

'Are you serious?'

'As serious as I am that this is the craziest fucking day of my life.' He tucks the envelope into his back pocket and looks me dead in the eye. 'What about the tour? Are you bailing on me?'

I shrug as he continues to stare at me. Finally, I nod.

'Yeah, I gotta stay here. My grandma will kill me if I let Senia have the baby alone.'

'Doing it for Grandma, huh?'

I try not to let him see the internal struggle going on inside me right now – the voice telling me that Grandma won't be around long enough to know if I leave Senia to go on tour.

'Yeah, let's just stick with that story for now,' I reply. 'I'm not used to this relationship bullshit.'

'Thanks, man,' he says and I congratulate him, because that's what you're supposed to do when your best friend is getting married to the person he's been in love with for six years. But something is off. He has a faraway look in his eyes, and I hope he's not thinking about the one person who's not here with him today. 'Hey, Claire is pregnant,' he says, and his smile returns. 'Don't tell anyone. I'm going to tell everyone at the reception.'

I can't help but grin like a crazy person as I slowly nod my head. 'You just had to outdo me, didn't you? Now what? I'm gonna have to get married on a fucking tightrope?'

'I'll be there to cut the rope.'

When we head back to the big tent to wait for Claire to make her big entrance, I don't have to wait very long before Senia comes walking in wearing a black dress that hugs her gorgeous body, her hair pulled back exposing her slender neck. She walks with such grace and confidence.

'You're beautiful,' I whisper, and she smiles as she hooks her arm in mine and we set off down the aisle.

Something about watching all your best friend's dreams come true in a single moment is really fucking emotional. I manage to keep my cool, but I understand why ladies cry at these things. I understand why Jake was crying during his vows. Weddings are intense.

Senia cries throughout Chris and Claire's entire wedding ceremony and she sobs uncontrollably when Chris, Claire, Jake, and Rachel all get on stage and sing 'Your Song.' When Chris and Claire break the big news about Claire's pregnancy to the crowd, I have to hold her to console her.

'This is the most beautiful wedding ever,' she says with a deep sigh, then she uses a fancy napkin to soak up her tears.

'Yours will be better.' She looks up at me in total disbelief. 'I promise.'

Chapter Twenty-Eight

Four Years Ago

Thirteen months ago, I walked into Mrs Langley's art class and my eyes settled on a skinny girl with dark hair sitting in the corner of the class. I knew from the moment I saw Ashley that she was the girl from my last day at Elaine's house. What I couldn't see just by looking at her slumped shoulders and round brown eyes was that she, like me, had never spoken to anyone about what happened that day. She told me later that the reason she was removed from her aunt's home was because her aunt died in a freak car accident the week after Ashley and I met. It turned out her aunt was the woman sitting in the corner of the bedroom that day. When I asked Ashley why she hadn't told anyone, she replied, 'Because she's dead now. She can't hurt me any more.'

But she was wrong. Dead or not, the memory of what

happened in that back bedroom on that day and in the days after I left Elaine's were like pieces of glass in Ashley's skin. If she kept still, didn't talk to anyone or do anything, she could just ignore them. But just the slightest movement, the littlest reminder, and the pain would come rushing back. Just a few months ago, she broke down in the middle of the mall when she saw a toddler in a stroller with her hair styled in pigtails.

Sometimes, she goes catatonic for hours at a time. Her adoptive parents have done everything to get her the help she needs, but she's refused to talk to anyone about what happened. Until I walked into that art classroom.

She was silent for four years until we found each other. Now, after thirteen months of sharing our secrets and learning to trust, it's all over with a single sentence.

'He makes me happier than you do.'

'Because he doesn't know you. I'm the only one who knows you.'

Her face has a blank quality; her eyes a remoteness that tells me she's bluffing. She doesn't want to do this.

I knew when Ashley moved into the dorms at Duke a month ago that things would be difficult for us. I thought we'd have a rough nine months, then everything would go back to normal once I graduate from high school next year. I've been making the thirty-minute drive out to see her three times a week. I guess it wasn't enough.

'I can't be with you any more. He's better for me. We're in the same classes and we like the same music and—'

'Music?'

The only music Ashley ever listens to are my band's songs, some of which I wrote for her, and the stuff I add to her iPod. She's told me repeatedly that my music is the only music she feels safe listening to. Apparently, the day I met Ashley at Elaine's was a trial run to see how Ashley would perform, and she passed the test. After I left Elaine's, her aunt was disappointed, but she insisted that Ashley could still entertain the johns with stripteases. Ashley effectively blocked out the memory of the music she was forced to strip to, but she was left with a crippling fear of one day encountering one of those songs.

'You're lying to yourself or you're lying to me. I can't figure out which one it is.'

She shakes her head adamantly. 'No, I'm not. I don't love you. I . . . I love him. He's better for me.'

'Stop saying that.'

'He is!' Her hand trembles as she jams it into the pocket of her jeans and pulls out the necklace I gave her three months ago when she graduated. She holds her palm out and the gold heart glints in the mottled September sunlight. 'I don't want this.'

'I don't want it either. It's yours.'

'Take it or I'll throw it away.'

'Then fucking throw it away.'

She stares at the necklace for a moment and her cool composure is beginning to evaporate. 'I don't want it. Why can't you understand? I don't want anything from you.'

That's when I realize she doesn't want the necklace because she wants to leave every trace of her past behind her. Not because she doesn't love me. If she didn't love me, she'd throw it away.

I turn around to walk away and she calls out to me. 'Tristan! Please take it!' I continue down the concrete path in the campus courtyard. 'Tristan!'

When I turn around, she seizes the opportunity to hurl the necklace at my face, then she spins around and runs off in the direction of the dorms. I pluck the necklace off the concrete and tuck it into my pocket. I think I always knew this would happen. Though I certainly did try, I knew nothing and no one could fill the hole in Ashley's soul. And I may never forgive myself for that.

Chapter Twenty-Nine

Senia

Recovering from the wedding – and hangover – of the century would be a lot easier if Tristan had his amazing steam room to sweat out the two bottles of vodka he drank last night. *Ugh!* Just the thought of it makes me sick. I'm glad I'm pregnant and I don't have to deal with hangovers for at least another eight months.

'So I take it we're not going to breakfast with everyone before they leave for their honeymoons?'

He grunts and, for a moment, I think this is his response. Then, 'You can go. I can't eat anything right now.'

I prop my head up on my elbow as I trace shapes on his bare back with my fingertip. 'Were you drunk while Chris and Claire were singing last night?'

'I don't remember,' he mutters, then he shifts a little and the way the muscles in his back flex under his skin is so sexy. 'Can you get me a bottle of water?'

'Yeah, and I'll order you the room service hangover cure.'

'What's that?'

'I don't know. Probably Gatorade and a butler to hold your puke bucket.'

I continue lightly stroking his back and he turns gingerly onto his side to face me. 'I don't need any of that shit. I just need you and some water.'

I slide out of bed and grab a couple of bottles of water out of the mini-bar. I set one down on the night-stand then I open the other and hand it to him. He guzzles half the bottle in one shot then he twists the cap back on and beckons me back into bed.

'I promised your dad I'd keep my dick in my pants while we're in Vegas.'

'*WHAT?*'

'He made me promise. But don't worry. I canceled tomorrow's flight. We're leaving tonight instead. We're not staying another night in this hotel room. Besides, I think the point is moot now that he knows you're pregnant.'

'What time is our flight?' He grins as he takes the bottle of water and lightly presses it against my bare belly. I suck in a sharp breath through my teeth. 'That's cold!'

'I know, unlike you,' he says, tossing the bottle onto

the floor as he lifts my camisole and leans in to take my nipple into his mouth.

All I can think of, as he uses his fingers to stimulate me, is those two minuscule sentences he uttered last night, which obviously meant nothing to him. *Yours will be better. I promise.*

I push him away and he looks confused. 'I have to take a shower,' I say, sliding off the bed again.

'I'll come with you.'

'No. I want to shower alone.'

He sits up in the bed looking even more stupefied. 'Did I do something wrong?'

'No, I'm just . . . I . . .' I roll my eyes at my inability to form a complete sentence. 'I think we should talk about what's going to happen when you go on tour.'

He reaches for the other bottle of water on the nightstand and shrugs. 'What's to talk about? I'm not going on tour. I'm staying here.'

'When did you decide this?'

'Last night.'

He stares at the gauze taped to his wrist for a moment, almost as if he can't remember getting the tattoo, then he rips it off. He gazes at his wrist for a moment then lets out a deep sigh before he chugs some more water.

'When were you going to tell me?' I ask as I approach the bed. I want to see that tattoo.

He watches me as I approach with one eyebrow cocked mischievously; he knows I want to see his new ink. He holds his wrist out for me to see and now *I'm* confused.

'I was going to tell you today, I guess.'

'What does one-two-three mean?'

'I'll tell you later. You're not ready.'

I turn to head back toward the bathroom. 'You need to tell me what time our flight is, so I can be ready.'

'I have a plane on standby until seven p.m. I was thinking we could join the mile-high club tonight.'

I stop at the bathroom door and look over my shoulder. The sly grin he's wearing is hot enough to burn a hole in those thousand-dollar sheets. Who cares about what he may or may not have said at the reception last night? The sexiest, sweetest, most complicated guy I've ever known just gave my best friend a house for her wedding gift and asked me to join the mile-high club. I'm thinking he kind of has the hots for me.

I beckon him with my finger and he chuckles as he slowly slides off the bed. But we never make it to the shower together, because the phone call Tristan receives at that moment changes everything.

Chapter Thirty

Nine Years Ago

I try not to cry as I ride my bike back to Grandma's house – my house – but I can't fight the tears. I don't know what I just did to that girl, but I know I hurt her; and I know that neither of us will ever be the same.

I keep my hoodie pulled low over my face despite the fact that it's a ferociously humid afternoon in the middle of September. Sweat drips down my face and neck. It even drips down my forearms and my hands begin to slip on the handgrips of my bike. But I'm hopeful that if anyone sees me crying on the corner of Avent Ferry and Gorman, they'll think it's just the unbearable heat that's reddened my eyes and moistened my cheeks.

I make it home a few minutes past three in the afternoon. Letting my bike drop onto the parched lawn, I race up the porch steps and throw open the front door without regard as to whether anyone is standing on the other side. The tiny air-conditioning unit that juts through the half-open window has done a pretty successful job of keeping the house cool and I quickly peel off my hoodie to let the cool air wash over my overheated skin.

'Tristan! You're soaking wet!' Grandma cries as she enters the living room from the kitchen, wringing her hands on a damp towel that hangs loosely from the pocket of her apron. 'And you're red as a lobster! Were you riding your bike in this heat? What – what's that on your T-shirt? Is that . . . blood? Are you hurt? Did your mother hurt you?'

For the briefest of seconds, I consider telling her everything. Then I think of that shotgun in my face, and the look on Grandma's face if she ever finds out what I've done, and I know I'll never tell.

'Got a bloody nose on the way over here,' I reply, smiling for the first time in weeks. 'I'm okay now.'

She tilts her head as she reaches up and brushes my sweaty hair away from my face. 'You're not going back there, are you?'

I shake my head, too afraid that if I speak something may slip out.

'Good.' She pulls the towel out of her apron pocket and drapes it over her shoulder. 'I just made some of your favorite lemon cookies and I'll make you a sandwich. You must be hungry. Go on and take a shower and get changed.'

She looks at me for a moment and I have a feeling she wants to say something too. Maybe Noah's mom has been here and she wants to reprimand me. Or maybe she somehow knows what happened at Elaine's. Either way, she doesn't say anything.

'I'm sorry, Grandma.'

'For what?'

'For leaving you.'

Something about these words gets to her and she bats her eyelashes to blink back the tears. 'You go on and get clean.' I turn to head for the bathroom, but she grabs my arm. 'I love you. You know that, don't you?' I nod and she responds with a nod. 'Go on now.'

As I make my way to the restroom, I peek into Grandma's bedroom to get a glimpse of Molly. She's sitting on Grandma's bed watching *The Lion King 2*, but she whips her head around at the sound of the door creaking open.

Her smile beams as she shouts my name four times in a row. 'I'm watching Simba. Wanna watch?'

'I'll be back in a few minutes.'

'No, don't go away,' she cries as I begin to close the bedroom door.

I open the door and she smiles again. 'Come on. You can watch Simba,' she says, patting the mattress for me to sit down. 'You can stay.'

I chuckle as I take a seat next to her and she wiggles with excitement. 'Thanks,' I whisper. *I think that's all I needed to hear.*

Chapter Thirty-One

I can hardly understand Molly through her sobs. I want to tell her to calm down, but I also want to tell her I'm sorry that I'm not there. She finally calms down enough to say that Grandma was coughing up blood this morning. Then she passed out in the shower and hit her shoulder on the bath faucet handle, cutting her shoulder very badly.

'She's on a respirator,' she whimpers. 'It's really bad. You need to come home.'

'I'll be there as soon as I can. Don't leave the hospital. Just stay there, okay?'

'Okay.'

Senia and I get dressed and leave our belongings behind. I'm the only one in the band that doesn't have an assistant, but that's because Jake and Chris's assistants have always been more than willing to provide their help free of charge. I'm sure one of them won't mind packing up my stuff and bringing it back to Raleigh. But, after this, I'll definitely have to get an assistant of my own. I can't pay other people's employees in sexual favors any more.

Luckily, the plane I chartered for Senia and me to fly back to North Carolina today is equipped for long flights and will get us there in a little more than five hours. Once the plane is in the air, Senia unfastens both of our seatbelts and leads me to the lounge area in the center of the plane. I don't have the heart to tell her that I'm not in the mood for sex right now, so I just go with it. She leads me through the lounge area and into a bedroom near the back of the plane.

'Lie down,' she says as she closes the door behind her.

I do as she says. I fully expect her to start stripping for me, but all she does is kick off her heels then she lies down next to me. She laces her fingers through mine as she stares at the curved ceiling.

'My grandma passed when I was ten. She lived with us from the day I was born until the day she died. When I lost her I thought that I was being punished for all the bad things I'd done. I was ten so that was a very long list of despicable things like pinching my sisters, lying to my parents, and cutting off my Barbie doll's head.' She takes a deep breath and I can't decide if she's trying to calm herself or gather strength. 'It took me a while to realize that my sisters' sins were much worse than my own and there was no way God would punish my sisters by taking my grandma's life. But before I figured that out, I went to my mom and told her I was afraid I'd killed Grandma with my petty crimes. She laughed and told me that Grandma didn't die for my sins. She died because she was too old.'

She turns to face me and I'm not sure I understand what she's getting at. 'My point is that even the people who love you, with all their good intentions, don't always know the right words to say in these kinds of moments. I wish I knew what to say to ease your mind. I wish I could say that your grandmother is going to be fine and that you'd actually believe it. I wish I could say that Molly's going to be fine. But I can't predict the future and something tells me that you don't want to hear meaningless words of comfort right now. So, I'm sorry that I don't know what to say. But if there's anything I can *do*, I'm all yours.'

I lean over and kiss her forehead then pull her closer so she can lie her head on my shoulder. 'You can just lie here with me.'

I turn my face into her hair and breathe in her scent. She still smells a little like the champagne that was practically raining down from the heavens after Chris and Claire made their big announcement yesterday. Everyone is so happy for them to have a child after everything they went through. I'm even happy for them. But I'm sure Senia probably felt a pang of longing for some of that excitement to be directed toward us.

I wasn't that drunk when I told her that her wedding would be better. When everything calms down with Grandma and Molly, and Senia and the baby are settled in with me in the condo Chris just offered me last night in exchange for the house I gave him . . . then I'll ask her to marry me and we'll be able to plan the kind of wedding she deserves. It won't be a surprise wedding, but I'll make sure to have plenty of other surprises planned for her along the way.

I glance at the tattoo on my wrist and smile as I realize I got this tattoo because it has three meanings. But now it has four.

Chapter Thirty-Two

The hospital parking lot is full at 7 p.m. on the first of January. Somehow, this doesn't surprise me. I'm sure there are dozens or hundreds of people who are here to grieve the loss or injury of a family member, but all I want is to push past all their grief and declare my grief more important than theirs.

How do I even begin to grieve when I can't accept what's happening?

We enter the intensive care unit and the woman behind the information desk directs us to my grandmother's room with a grave expression. Why can't she muster a cheerful expression, just for this single moment? Why do I have to bear the brunt of her pity? I'm sure she gets so much bad news all day; it must be difficult to appear to be anything other than completely exhausted.

When Senia and I enter the critical care room at WakeMed, my head nearly explodes at the sight of Elaine and a man I assume is her new boyfriend standing at Grandma's bedside. Molly is seated in a chair on the other side of the bed next to a woman with grayish-brown hair and a purple sweater who appears to be taking notes on a clipboard.

'What's going on?'

Molly whips her head around at the sound of my voice and she runs to me, throwing her arms around my waist. 'They're saying I have to live with her.'

'What? That's ridiculous.' I pull away from Molly as the woman in the purple sweater turns around to look at me. I look straight at her as I speak the next sentence. 'Molly has never lived with Elaine and she never will.'

'I'm sorry, Mr . . . ?'

The woman rises from her chair and holds her hand out to me as if I'm going to shake it. 'I'm Molly's older brother and I can take care of Molly until our grandma is better.'

She looks slightly perplexed by this statement. 'You're . . . Tristan?' she asks as she continues to shake my hand.

'Yes.'

'I'm Mrs Rathbone. The social worker assigned to your sister's case. We just need to make sure your sister is taken care of while your grandmother is in the hospital.' She pushes the chair aside so I can squeeze in next to Grandma's bed, then she continues to write something on her clipboard. 'Molly told me she would rather live with you, but your mother does have the authority in this situation. Is it true that there is no custody agreement that says you or your grandmother have custody of Molly? Because, if so, I need to know if there is any reason why I should believe that your mother is not equipped to care for her?'

I laugh through gritted teeth as I keep my eyes locked on Elaine's skinny face. 'She's not my mother and the reasons why she shouldn't be allowed to call herself Molly's mother are endless.'

'I'm not sure I understand. Do you care to explain that in more detail?'

Molly knows nothing about what happened the three weeks I lived with Elaine when I was twelve. She doesn't know the things I did and I hope she never does.

'I can't say more than that. But, come on, she hasn't taken care of her own children for twelve years. All Molly knows about her is that she's an addict.'

'Recovering addict,' Elaine interjects. 'I'm clean. Right, Joe?'

The guy standing next to her with his shaggy blond mustache and green and white trucker hat nods. 'Clean as a . . . she's real clean.'

'You've gotta be kidding me?' I say, addressing the social worker. 'These two have about as much parental instincts as a fucking dingo. You can't make Molly go with them.'

'Please watch the language,' Mrs Rathbone says, looking annoyed with my choice of words.

'Fine. I'll watch the language, if you promise me that Molly is coming home with me tonight.'

Elaine clears her throat to get everyone's attention before she speaks. 'Mrs Rathbone, I hate to tell you this in front of everyone, but Tristan has a history of violence. I don't think Molly should be allowed to live with him.'

'Are you fucking kidding me?' I roar, incensed by this ridiculous accusation. 'If you want to get into our histories, we can do that, but don't you dare make up baseless lies to satisfy whatever agenda you're trying to see played out here. Is it the *house* you want? You can have it. You don't need Molly to get the fucking house. I'll give it to you. Just leave us the fuck alone!'

Molly squats down next to me and covers her face as she sobs. Mrs Rathbone appears conflicted as to whether she should believe Elaine's accusations or if she should go with her gut, and Molly's request, to come home with me.

I kneel next to Molly and place my hand on her shoulder. 'I've got a place in Chapel Hill. I know it's far from your friends, but I'm sure Jackie will help us so you won't have to change schools.'

'I don't want to leave. All my friends live in Raleigh. Why do *I* have to leave? Why can't you just move back in?'

I glance up at Senia and I know she'd probably tell me to do whatever is best for Molly, but I don't think becoming embroiled in a custody battle with

Elaine over my grandmother's house is what's best for her. Molly's not thinking. Besides, I highly doubt that it's just Grandma's house Elaine wants. I've been padding her bank accounts for months and Molly is probably listed as the beneficiary on those accounts. I'm sure Elaine knows that Grandma wouldn't leave me anything I didn't need – and there's nothing I need any more. I'll hire an estate lawyer first thing tomorrow morning.

Even stronger than my desire to keep Elaine's hands off Grandma's assets is my desire to not live in the house I grew up in. I can't imagine waking up there every day, feeling as if I've stepped into an even more depressing version of *Groundhog Day*. I sure as hell don't want to raise my child in that tiny two-bedroom house where Elaine grew up. And there's no way I'm going to live in a place where Elaine feels she can visit us every other day.

'How about this? We'll scrap the place in Chapel Hill and we'll get something near Grandma's,' I say and Molly looks up at me with interest.

Her eyes are puffy and glistening, but her face lights up instantly as she realizes I'm serious. 'You would do that?'

'I'll do anything to keep you away from her.'

A crease forms between her eyebrows, and I know she's wishing I wasn't so angry with Elaine. Her expression makes me think of the times I used to read her to sleep. I'd stroke her eyebrows sometimes. They were wispy and soft, and she had a habit of scrunching them up while she slept. I thought if I smoothed her brow, the nightmares would go away.

Mrs Rathbone clears her throat to interrupt our discussion. 'Unfortunately, Molly will have to go with her mother until we can find some kind of living will or custody agreement that precludes her mother. Since it's New Year's Day, we'll have to wait until tomorrow to settle this. It will probably only be a couple of nights. Or, if she prefers, we could put her in a temporary foster care facility.'

I grab Molly's hand and pull her up so we're both standing. 'No, you don't understand. She's not going anywhere with her or any damn stranger. Ever. Not for any amount of days or seconds.'

'Well, I'm afraid that it doesn't work that way. She needs to go somewhere.'

'Yeah, I'm—'

I point at Elaine and she stops speaking. 'Don't say it. You're not her mother. You haven't been her mother since she was a year old and probably even before that. So you can quit this little act.'

'I *am* her mother and she won't be staying with me a couple of nights. She's coming to live with me.'

This is too much for me to handle right now when I'm hungover and Grandma is lying in a bed four feet away from me with a machine breathing for her. I run my hand over my face and take a deep breath. I need a drink.

'Maybe she can stay with Jackie until you guys settle this?' Senia offers.

'Who's Jackie?' Rathbone asks.

I can't believe I never thought of that. Chris's mother, Jackie Knight, hasn't taken in any foster children since Claire came to their house, like, six years ago. I wonder if there's some kind of license or certification she needs to maintain to be a foster parent. If so, she's definitely let that lapse since then.

'Jackie is the mother of a friend of mine. She used to take in foster children a few years ago.'

'That doesn't change the fact that her mother wants her and we have no evidence of wrongdoing on her part,' Rathbone replies, and I want to wipe the sympathetic look off her face. 'Unless you have specific accusations to make against her.'

I glance at Senia and Molly then I close my eyes. I wince as the images assault me. *The woman in the corner smiling. The black tears running down Ashley's cheeks and soaking the pillow. The blood on the sheets.*

I shake my head and open my eyes. 'Let me at least say goodbye to her in private.'

Molly looks horrified as I pull her into the corridor. 'You can't let me go with her.'

I shush her as I continue to drag her away from the room. Senia walks next to me, but I can't bring myself to look at her. I don't want to know what she thinks about what I'm doing.

'You can't do this. This could be kidnapping,' Senia

whispers as we turn the corner and the sliding exit doors appear at the end of the corridor.

'I can't let her go with Elaine.'

'It's just a couple of nights. Don't do something you'll regret the rest of your life for a couple of nights.'

'You don't know shit about Elaine, so you should just shut up about things you obviously don't understand,' I bark at her.

The moment we reach the exit doors and they slide open for us, a deep voice shouts, 'Stop right there, sir!'

The sight of the two security guards in their gray uniforms throws me into a panic. I grip Molly's hand tighter and race outside into the parking lot, which is now covered by a fresh dusting of snow.

'Tristan, stop!' Senia shouts, but I don't look back.

I'll never look back.

Chapter Thirty-Three

'You're crazy!' Molly shouts as I peel out of the hospital parking. 'What if they arrest you? Then I'll have to live with her forever!'

'They're not going to arrest me because I didn't take you against your will.'

'I've watched enough *Law and Order* to know that doesn't mean shit. You're so stupid.'

I turn into a residential tract and turn on my GPS to help me get out of here from a different street. The first place they'll probably look for us is my house, but I've watched a lot of cop shows, too. I'm not that stupid. And no one other than me, Chris, and Claire know the address to Chris's condo. They're on their honeymoon. I'm sure they won't mind if Molly and I crash there for a few days until we get this sorted out, or until Grandma wakes up.

Oh, God. What am I going to do if she wakes up and we're not there? What did I get us into?

I ask my phone to Google estate lawyers and I leave

voicemail messages for four of them while I drive. I try not to drive fast, but I know that if they do put out an all-points bulletin on my car – I highly doubt it – that my British electric sports car is too easily recognizable. I need to get to Chris's condo fast.

As I turn onto Franklin Street, surrounded by all the UNC hangouts, I think of Senia. This is the home that Senia and I are supposed to move into so she can be closer to campus. I hope I haven't completely fucked that up.

'Thank God,' I whisper as I pull up in front of the condo high-rise and find they have underground parking. I wonder if Chris will respond if I text him asking for the code to enter the underground lot. I shoot off a text, ignoring the notification of a voicemail from Senia, as I drive across the street to the Quickee Mart and hide my car between a couple of trucks.

Me: *Can I get the code to your underground parking? I'm showing Senia the place and I don't want to park my car on the street.*

'Who are you texting?' Molly asks as she looks around the car.

The parking lot is pretty full. It's about 8 p.m. on New Year's Day. People are probably still celebrating the New Year. I have nothing to celebrate tonight.

'No one.'

Chris: *49852. Use space number G45. Door code is 8992.*

By the time I pull into space number G45 in the underground lot, the snow has transformed to freezing rain. The lot is heated, but it's not enough to stave off the chill that penetrates through the slats of the gated entrance and the fabric of the white dress shirt I wore with my tux last night. It will probably be even colder tonight without Senia in my bed.

I should call her and apologize, but I don't know if she's with those security guards, or the cops. I don't want to risk bringing her into this. I just need to find out who drafted Grandma's will so I can get my hands on a copy of it. If Grandma Flo left everything to Molly, then I can present that as a motive for Elaine's sudden interest in getting custody of her. And, if necessary, I'll tell them everything about her twisted ways.

Once we enter the condo, Molly heads straight for the kitchen. 'I'm hungry.'

'Get whatever you want.'

She opens up the refrigerator as I look around. The condo is impeccably clean and modern, like it's hardly been lived in. Of course, Chris and Claire have lived here less than a month. It's nice. Senia would like it here.

'They don't have anything except Capri-Sun, bacon, and water,' Molly calls from the kitchen.

'I'll order you some pizza,' I call back to her over my

shoulder, unable to tear my gaze away from the view through the glass doors leading out to the balcony. The way the raindrops glisten in the moonlight is mesmerizing.

I was accustomed to snow when I lived with Elaine in Maine. She used to tell me to get my coat on and go outside and play in the snow. I remember the neighbor delivering me onto our doorstop and ringing the bell after he found me in his backyard with blue fingers and lips. I had strayed onto his property, which was a good thing because Elaine didn't even remember how long I'd been out there. She thanked the guy, and all my eight-year-old mind could think was that maybe I could win a world record for rolling in the snow for six hours. It doesn't snow that much in Raleigh. And despite all the animosity I feel toward Elaine now, I can't help but long for the snow when it's gone.

'Why do you hate her?'

I turn around and find Molly sitting on the sofa with her shoes off and her feet propped up on the coffee table.

'Don't put your feet on the table. This isn't our house.'

She rolls her eyes as she removes her feet. 'You didn't answer my question. Why do you hate Elaine so much?'

'I've already told you. She's a worthless junkie who treated us and Grandma like trash.'

I sit next to her and the first thing I notice is that

there's no TV in the living room. Chris and Claire must be getting it on a lot in their new place.

'She did something to you, didn't she?'

'What? Who?'

'Don't play dumb with me.'

I kick my shoes off and put my feet up on the coffee table. 'Let's eat first. Then I'll tell you everything.'

Chapter Thirty-Four

Senia

From perfect to jerk in less than two seconds. The only guy ever to tell me to shut up was Tar Heel point guard Kevin Brown during a particularly wild frat party my freshman year, and I slapped him then pissed in his lap. I was rip-roaring drunk at the time and I needed to pee really badly, but, still, *no one* tells me to shut up.

'Ma'am, do you know where they might have run off to?'

The security guard's smooth brown skin comes into focus. 'What?'

'Your friend? Do you know where he may have taken the girl?'

I shake my head. 'He didn't take the girl. That's his fucking sister.'

'Ma'am, we're just trying to keep the girl safe. There's no need to use that kind of language.'

The other security guard next to him tilts his head as he stares at me with a skeptical expression on his boxy face. He's probably judging me – judging *all of us* in his head. He thinks we're in this situation because we're trash or because we're one of those families that's addicted to drama. One of those families . . . *Did I just refer to myself as part of Tristan's family?*

Holy shit. I need to find Tristan and Molly.

'I'll be right back,' I say, pushing box-head out of my way as I stalk off toward the main hospital entrance.

I need to call Tristan and I need to call a cab so I can go get my car. I dial Tristan's number, but he doesn't answer. Tristan hardly ever has his ringer on. Most of the time, he doesn't even have the phone set to vibrate. It's just completely silent. He doesn't like to be interrupted when he's practicing or socializing. But I made him set the phone to vibrate when we got off the plane earlier, in case Molly or Grandma Flo called him. If he's not answering, he's probably just ignoring me. Asshole.

I get his voicemail greeting and I try to think of what I'm going to say during the brief seconds while I listen to his voice: *I'm not available. Leave a message. Beeeeep.*

'I . . . I think there's something you're not telling me and I just want to know how I can help.'

I hang up the phone and try not to cry as I think of the little human swimming inside me right now. He or she is doomed to have a fiery temper with Tristan and me as parents. I wonder if she'll have Tristan's golden-brown hair or gray eyes or if he'll be a clone of me, the way Abigail is a clone of Claire.

I wish Claire weren't on her honeymoon. I need her. I need to know that this isn't the end. I need to know that being this scared is normal.

I wipe the tears from my eyes as I walk past the Heart Center and Children's Hospital where I brought Claire to see Abigail almost three months ago. I think I'm finally beginning to understand Claire more than I did just a few weeks ago. I just wish I could understand why Tristan is the way he is with his mother. There has to be more to his hatred than a tragic story of abandonment.

I open the browser app on my phone and begin searching for taxi companies. The smell of fresh snow in the courtyard is such a calming scent. I wish I could bottle it up and take it home with me. I close my eyes and breathe it in, let it wash away the doubts I have about my future with Tristan. I don't see the patch of ice on the concrete stairs. One second I'm falling, falling through the smell of snow. The next second, everything is gone.

Chapter Thirty-Five

'I got tired of being *the man of the house*,' I begin as I set my empty plate on top of the pizza box. 'I was twelve years old and you were four. Grandma did the best she could, but she was struggling with money because she was living off the savings and insurance money from when Grandpa died. Grandma didn't know, but I had started stealing stuff from stores to sell to people at school for money. I told her I didn't need her to make me school lunches – I thought I was too cool for that – and I told her not to give me any lunch money. But it all became too much. I started to resent Grandma for being so damn cheap and poor.'

I clutch my stomach as the guilt twists my insides. I've made more mistakes than I can count, but not being happy with the life Grandma provided for us was the biggest.

I take a deep breath and continue. 'Then I got into trouble when one of my friends' parents found a bunch of watches we'd stolen. I thought that was it. I was going down. My grades had been slipping for a while. I hated coming home every day and knowing that I was going to have to keep you entertained while Grandma spent two or three hours cooking and cleaning. I just wanted to hang out and do bad shit with my friends, but Grandma wanted me to be *a responsible young man*.'

Molly's golden-brown eyes are locked on me as she listens, rapt with attention as I prepare to tell her everything I probably should have told her years ago. I think I never wanted Molly to know because I was afraid of Grandma finding out. I don't think Grandma would judge me, but I think it would destroy her to know that the daughter she still loves very much would do something like that.

'I showed up at Elaine's house and, at first, she didn't know what to do with me. She put me to work cutting the lawn and delivering packages, which I assumed were filled with drugs.'

I close my eyes and grit my teeth as I think of the fear that twisted my stomach into knots as I made those deliveries. But even with all the fear that consumed me, there was still an element of excitement to it. And the money was pretty good: $25 per delivery, which usually took less than an hour to complete.

'I thought to myself: I can do this. I can deliver stuff on my bike. It was summer. If I weren't at Elaine's, I'd probably be riding my bike around town every day anyway. But this way, I was making money.' I look at Molly and she's biting the corner of her lip nervously, like she knows what's coming. 'But the deliveries didn't last. She came to me and told me she found a place for us to live – just her and me. She said she needed to make enough money for the first month's rent and deposit. We needed two thousand dollars and we could leave. All I had to do is have sex with a girl who actually *wanted* to have sex with me.'

Molly's face contorts as she begins to cry quietly.

'She told me that we wouldn't be able to get the apartment in time just doing deliveries. It would only be a few times and we'd make enough money to leave . . . I told her I'd never had sex with anyone and I didn't want to do it, but she wouldn't let it go. She had a couple of her friends talk to me about it. And one of the younger girls who lived there – I think her name was Cecily, or something like that – she was a heroin addict who was actually kind of pretty. Anyway, she got me drunk and we started making out. Then she just got up and left and I thought maybe I did want to have sex. Maybe it wouldn't be so bad.'

I draw in a deep breath and I close my eyes so I don't have to see Molly's face when I continue.

'I had sex with the first girl that night. I never found out her name, but I didn't need to know it. We were both there for the same thing, to get paid. Only thing was she was getting paid in drugs and Elaine was getting paid by . . . by the guys who came in and watched us.'

Molly has the heels of her hands pressed into her

eyelids and I can't bring myself to touch her to comfort her. I feel filthy, as if the guilt is seeping through my skin. The shame is something I've lived quietly with, but talking about it now . . . it's so fucking loud and vile. I don't want to go on, but I know I can't stop now. She needs to know.

'The first two times were horrible, but the last girl . . .' I let go a deep sigh as the first sign of tears form in my eyes. 'You remember Ashley, don't you?'

She uncovers her eyes and looks at me with pure shock in her eyes. 'Ashley?'

I cover my face to hide the tears. 'I hate myself for what I did.'

'Oh my God, Tristan. You . . . you've been living with this and I never knew? All this time, I thought you were mad at Elaine because she's a piece-of-shit junkie.'

She grabs my hands and pries my fingers away from my face. 'Don't do that,' I say, pushing her away.

She sniffs loudly, her lip trembling as she looks me in the eye. 'I hate her.'

'Don't say that. She didn't do anything to you. That anger is mine to carry, not yours.'

'Yes, it is! She hurt you and now I'll never be able to look at her again. I hate her! Oh my God, I hate her so much.'

The mixture of rage and agony in Molly's face kills me. I don't want her to be consumed by this the way I have been. Maybe I shouldn't have told her anything.

'Hey,' I say, grabbing her arm to turn her toward me. 'Don't let her do this to you. She did it to me for way too many years . . . It's time to let it go.'

Her nose is starting to drip from crying so hard and I get a strange urge to use my sleeve to wipe it clean, the way I used to when she was a kid and I was too lazy to get a tissue. I get up from the sofa and head for the kitchen to get a paper towel. When I come back, her eyes are closed and her head is leaned against the back of the sofa. Her chest stutters as she draws in a deep breath.

I tap her arm to get her attention and she takes the paper towel from me. She shakes her head as she wipes her face clean.

'Take me back to the hospital. I'll go with a foster family for a couple of days. I just don't want you to get in trouble.'

'You're not going to live with strangers. You're staying with me tonight.'

'You can't pretend that nothing is going to happen to you if you keep me here.' She turns to me and fixes me with an intense glare. 'And you need to apologize to Senia and tell her everything, or I'm not living with you.'

I can't help but chuckle at this threat. 'You really like her, don't you?'

'What's not to like? She puts you in your place and she has the best drunk stories.'

'She does.'

I pull my phone out of my pocket to listen to Senia's voicemail, when I notice I have a text from Elaine.

Elaine: *Your girlfriend fell outside the hospital. She's in the emergency room. It don't look good.*

Chapter Thirty-Six

I didn't know love had a sound. I know that Senia's tongue tastes like Tic Tacs, and, to me, that tastes like love. I know her neck smells like Ralph Lauren perfume. And I know the softness of her skin on every part of her body. But I guess you don't really know the *sound* of love until you hear the sound of your heartbeat pounding in your ears when you're worried about the one person you hope you never have to live without. The *two* people you can't live without.

Molly and I race to the underground lot and jump into my car. The battery indicator on the dashboard is extremely low. I didn't leave the car charging before I went to Vegas, then I drove the car from Cary to Raleigh, and to Chapel Hill. I won't get far on what little charge I have left on this battery.

Fuck it. I have to at least try.

If I punch the accelerator too hard, the battery will wear down faster. So, as difficult as it is to restrain myself, I try to drive like Grandma Flo. I can't fucking believe I left Senia there alone. *What the hell is wrong with me?*

The battery indicator goes down again and now it says I have twenty-one miles left on this charge. I punch in WakeMed on the GPS and my heart drops when I see it's still twenty-three miles away. I have to find a shortcut somewhere.

'Molly, Google shortcuts. Look for open fields or parking lots that I can cut through. Hurry up!'

She pulls her phone out of her pocket and her fingers fly across the screen as she attempts to find a shorter path to the hospital.

'I don't know! I don't know what any of this means. I don't know how to read a map!' she cries.

I take the phone from her hand and attempt to keep my eyes on the road as I also search the map on her phone for open spaces. There's nothing I can cut through. The path to the hospital is almost a straight line. I'm fucked.

Twenty-seven minutes later, I pull my car into a Wal-Mart parking lot just in time to get it into a parking space before it dies. I yank the key out of the ignition and turn to Molly.

'As soon as I get out of the car, lock the doors. Call Jackie to pick you up. She should be home from Vegas. And if she's not, call Elaine.'

I leave her my key so she can arm the car alarm, then I take off running in the direction of the hospital. The buildings and trees on New Bern Avenue are a blur in my peripheral vision as I haul ass down the sidewalk. And at that moment, it dawns on me. I should have responded to Elaine's text to ask her to tell the hospital staff that Senia's pregnant. *Fuck!*

I have to get to her. I have to tell them so they can make sure everything's okay with the baby.

I'm thankful for all those morning workouts in my home gym because, by the time I reach the emergency-room entrance, I'm on such an adrenaline high, I still feel as if I could run a marathon if that's what it took to get to her. I tumble through the sliding doors and into the emergency room and I'm not sure I'm making sense. But the nurse must understand all my frantic words and gestures because she leads me into Bay B of the emergency room. The curtains are drawn on most of the beds, and I want to tear them all open to find her, but I restrain myself. The nurse is looking straight ahead, so I have a feeling Senia is in the bed near the back of the room where the curtain is open.

I walk a few steps ahead of her and when we reach the last bed, the space is empty. There's no bed or Senia.

'Where is she?'

The nurse looks confused. 'Hmm . . . They must have moved her.'

She turns around and heads back toward the nurses' station. 'Why would they move her? Is she okay? What does her file say?'

She looks at the file in her hand and flips through a

couple of pages. 'She was unconscious when she came in. She presented with what looks like a broken finger and a pretty bad laceration and contusion on the back of her head.'

'And the baby?'

'She's pregnant?'

'Yes! I thought I told you that.'

'No, you said you were her husband, but you never said she was pregnant.'

She power-walks the rest of the way to the nurses' station and types something on her computer. When she finds the information she's looking for, she dials a number on the desk phone.

'Yes, please let Dr Vartanian know that the patient is pregnant. Yes, thank you.' She turns to me before I can say anything. 'They stitched up her head, but it's lucky you got here when you did. They were about to give her a CAT scan. They'll have to examine her first; make sure the baby's okay.'

'When will I hear from them? Can I go there to be with her?'

'You can wait in the waiting room right outside there and I'll let you know as soon as I hear anything.'

I heave a deep sigh because I don't want to believe the words I'm about to say. 'My grandmother is in ICU – Florence Pollock. You can reach me in her room.'

I trudge through the hospital corridors, feeling so completely broken, it doesn't even occur to me that I won't find Elaine here. Grandma and the steady sound of air being pushed in and out of her lungs are the only things to keep me company now. Elaine must have gone to pick up Molly. I text Molly to make sure she's okay, and she texts me back right away to say that Jackie never answered so she ran to the hospital right behind me. She's just walking through the parking lot now.

I shake my head at her defiance as I take a seat in the chair next to Grandma's bed. I can still feel the blood pulsing in my legs from the run over here. Stroking the soft skin on her arm, I try to think of something to say to her. What do you say to the person you never properly thanked for saving your life?

'Grandma?' I whisper. 'I don't know if you can hear me, but I want you to know that I'm sorry I didn't thank you enough for everything you've done for me and Molly. I wish I would have told you this before I left to Vegas yesterday, but you're the best mom I could have ever asked for. You made me believe that people could be good; that life could be good. You taught me that hard work isn't always fun, but it always pays off.'

The beeping of the machine next to me is soothing as I think of my favorite memory of Grandma. 'Remember my ninth birthday? We had just moved down here from Maine and, man, the weather is so much hotter here in August than it is over there. You invited a bunch of the neighborhood kids – kids I didn't even know – and we all played hide-and-seek in the backyard for hours. When it was time for the cake, you told me I had to count to three before I made a wish. And you know what I wished for? You'll get a kick out of this. I wished for Molly to stop throwing up on me.'

I whip my head around at the sound of footsteps. It's Molly, and Elaine is standing at the doorway. Molly closes the door on Elaine and I'm so thankful for Molly's strength.

Tears stream down her face as she pulls up a chair next to me. 'Did I stop barfing on you?'

I wrap my arm around her and she rests her head on my shoulder. 'Yeah, you did, but I think it had more to do with the fact that Grandma knew how to take better care of you.' But that didn't stop me from believing that counting to three was the secret to making all my wishes come true.

Chapter Thirty-Seven

When I walk into Senia's room, she's awake and staring at the ceiling. She tries to turn her head at the sound of my voice, but the pain stops her. I rush to her side and I don't care if she can see the tears in my eyes.

'I'm so sorry,' I whisper as I lean in to kiss her forehead. 'I'm so sorry I left you behind.'

I grab her hand and she squeezes it against her chest. 'The baby's gone.'

'I know.' I smooth her dark hair away from her face and kiss her forehead again. 'I'm sorry I wasn't here for you.'

She shakes her head and more tears slip loose from the corners of her eyes. 'It's not your fault. I shouldn't have worn those stupid heels.'

'Don't say that. Don't even think that.' I squeeze her hand and clench my jaw as I try to stay strong for her.

'Where did you go?' she whispers. 'Where's Molly?'

'Baby, I need to tell you something.' Her eyes squeeze

shut and I lean in to kiss the tears on her temple. 'I need to tell you everything.'

And I tell her everything; so much more than I told Molly. I want her to know the darkest parts of me, because those are the parts that will make her want to leave. When I'm done, her nails are digging into my hand. I gently pry her fingers loose and brush the tears from her cheeks.

'I always thought that if anyone knew the truth, if anyone knew the real me, and the things I'm capable of, no one would love me, and what's the point of letting someone fall in love with a lie? So it was easy – I never fell in love and I never spoke to anyone about it until today. I never had a reason to. But you give me so many reasons to do things I never thought I could do. I just want to be better for you. I want to be better in your eyes.'

'I hate that bitch now and I'm so sorry I questioned you when you left.' I chuckle a little at this passionate response, but Senia's face is full of anguish. 'Now I know why you go from perfect to jerk in two seconds flat. But I'm sorry I ever doubted you. And I'm sorry if I ever doubt you in the future. I'm sure this will come as a total surprise to you, but I'm not perfect either. I mean, I'm practically defective now.'

'You're not defective. Your CAT scan said your head was still perfect.' I brush my thumb across her cheekbone and she latches onto my hand. 'Perfect in every way.'

‘I’m not talking about my head,’ she says, heaving a deep, exhausted sigh.

‘I know. But you didn’t lose the baby because you’re defective. It happened because life isn’t perfect. Not you.’

‘Lie with me?’

It takes me a moment to figure out how to lower the side rail on her bed, then she carefully turns onto her side so I can scoot in next to her. She lays the side of her head on my chest as I wrap my arm around her shoulders. I stroke her arm for a while, trying to pretend I can’t hear her crying.

‘I had names picked out already.’

‘What names?’

‘Kalen for a girl and Cross for a boy.’

‘I like Kalen, but I can’t agree to Cross.’

She breathes in deeply and I can feel the trembling in her chest against my chest. ‘What boys’ names do you like?’

‘I was kind of hoping we could have a Junior.’

‘But that’s so cliché.’

‘And Cross is not a cliché? Didn’t you say you were reading a book with a character named Cross? We’re not naming our kids after characters.’

‘Didn’t your mom name you after Tristan and Isolde?’

‘That doesn’t count. Our son will be named Tristan. That is my only request.’

She’s silent for a moment before she speaks again. ‘How’s your grandma?’

I tighten my grip on her shoulder as I think of what the doctor told me shortly before I came in here. 'The doctor said that he doesn't think she's going to come off the respirator soon; or, possibly, at all. And . . . and even if she does come off, she'll be in a lot of pain.'

Senia uses the sheet to wipe the tears from her face this time. 'Do you know what you're going to do?'

'We have to find her will tomorrow. I'm pretty sure that she's specified she doesn't want to stay on any kind of life support. She told us she wants to go quietly. But I don't think I'm ready for that.'

The pain wells up inside me and I try my hardest not to conjure up images in my mind of a life without Grandma Flo.

'I don't know what this will do to Molly,' I continue. 'I don't know how I'm going to take care of her for the next five years until she becomes an adult. I don't know the first thing about raising a teenager.'

'You'll figure it out. You didn't know anything about playing the bass when Chris came to you and asked if you wanted to start a band, and look at you now.'

I grab her hand and bring it to my lips. Her fingers smell like antibacterial hand soap. I hold the backs of her fingers against my cheek to feel the softness of her skin, then I lay a kiss on the inside of her wrist.

'What am I going to do with you? You always know what to say. You're always outsmarting me.'

She finally lets go a small chuckle, which is quickly followed by a small whimper. 'You did beat me at hide-and-seek,' she replies, her voice once again muffled by grief. Then she squeezes out a few words that are completely unrelated and totally unexpected. 'I thought when I told you I was pregnant, you would tell me to get lost.'

I want to ask her why she would think that, but, if I were her, I would have thought the same thing about me five weeks ago. I would not have imagined myself inviting a pregnant girl to live with me and I definitely would never have imagined myself confessing my love to her and talking about weddings.

She clutches the front of my shirt in her fist. 'I thought when you found out about the baby today, you'd leave me here alone.'

'What? I . . . don't even know what to say to that. You thought I'd just abandon you like that?'

'I'm sorry. I just had this horrible feeling that the only reason you were with me was because of the baby.'

'I know you can't move your head to look at me right now, but listen to these words carefully and never forget them . . . I'm sorry I used to be the kind of person who would do something like that. And I will never abandon you. I wasn't with you because of the baby. The baby was just the icing on a very fucking delicious cake. Do you believe me?'

'Well, when you put it that way, what choice do I have?'

'You have no choice. You're stuck with me, for worse or for worse.'

'I'm so tired.' I move to slide out of the bed, but she holds tightly to my shirt. 'Don't go.'

I loosen my grip on her shoulder and adjust my position a little so she can get more comfortable. 'So what do we do now?'

'How about we vow to never screw up the way we did outside Yogurtland?'

'I can't promise that. What happened outside Yogurtland was one of the smartest mistakes I've made in a long time. I hope I get to make those kinds of mistakes with you for . . . forever.'

Chapter Thirty-Eight

After spending a restless night in the hospital, trying to decide if I should sit next to Grandma or lie with Senia, they finally discharge Senia at 6 a.m. and she calls her sister, Maribel, to pick her up. The look on her face as she sits down in the passenger seat of her sister's car breaks me apart. I kneel next to her and cradle her face in my hands, resting my forehead against hers.

'I'll do whatever it takes to make this right,' I say as I plant a kiss on her nose and release her. I lower my hand to her abdomen and she lays her hand over mine.

She bites her lip as it begins to tremble. 'I know.'

It turns out the third lawyer I left a message for was the one who drew up Grandma's will. He calls me at 9.06 a.m., as if I'm the first person he decided to call after listening to all his voicemail messages. That, or I was the only message he had. Either way, I'm just glad to hear his voice. I'm even more glad when he tells me that I can come in that morning to go over the will.

After waiting around for nearly two hours for a second social worker to show up at the hospital, Elaine decided she couldn't wait any more and left before the social worker got there. When the social worker, Mrs Greenlee, arrived, she was more than happy to allow Molly to stay with me until everything is sorted out with Grandma's will. It was less paperwork for her and I think she could see by the weariness in our faces that we had been through enough.

I send Elaine a text telling her to arrive at the lawyer's office by 10 a.m. or I won't hesitate to dredge up a witness to her sick crimes. I would never, in a million years, contact Ashley to ask her to talk about what happened nine years ago just for my sake. But, if I had to, I wouldn't hesitate to do it for Molly.

Elaine strolls into the waiting room at Lynch & Mellman, LLC, trailed closely by her new boyfriend, Joe, and his pedo-stache. Like I was ever going to allow Molly to go anywhere with those two. She's wearing sunglasses indoors at 10.07 a.m. and carrying a carton of milk with a straw sticking out. Her gait is loose and weighed down, but it isn't until she starts scratching her neck and scalp that I realize she's high.

I clench my jaw to keep from saying something I'll regret before we read the will, then I stand from the chair and head for the receptionist's desk. 'We're ready,' I tell her and she smiles shyly at me as she tucks her blonde hair behind her ear.

'Where's Molly?' Elaine asks in that nasally slurred

tone I thought I'd never hear again after I moved out of Grandma's house.

'At home, where she should be,' I reply as the receptionist leads us down a hallway to Jonah Lynch's office.

This is a tiny law office, but I didn't expect much for an estate planning lawyer in Raleigh. Still, something about the quaintness of this space makes me uneasy. It could just be knowing that Grandma was in here four months ago discussing what she wanted to happen after her death. She's not even gone and I can already feel her presence everywhere.

We enter Jonah's office and he rounds the desk to greet us near the door. The office is bigger than I expected and it has a decent view of the eastern parking lot where the sun would rise if he ever came in early or stayed way too late; not that I have any illusions of estate lawyers being *that* passionate about their work. But I hope Jonah has more than a few drops of compassion in him because I may need it if Elaine sets me off today.

'Please have a seat,' Jonah says, motioning to the two chairs in front of his mahogany desk.

He looks fairly young, maybe early thirties, with neat brown hair and a blue suit that looks like it may even have been tailored for him. I don't know why, but I trust him just by looking at him. I hope that's the way Grandma felt when she came here.

'Maybe he should wait outside,' I say, pointing my thumb at Joe. 'He's not family.'

'Don't be such a prick. He can stay,' Elaine slurs and Jonah looks uncomfortable. He can probably tell she's not sober.

'Fine,' I reply, keeping my eyes on Jonah's face. 'Can we just get this over with?'

Jonah nods as he lifts a blue folder from his desk and opens it up. 'First of all, let me say that I'm very sorry for what you're going through.'

Elaine lets out a slow, low-pitched whimper as she begins to cry. Jonah looks to me for guidance and I nod my head for him to continue, but I'm angry. I'm angry at myself that I can hear Elaine's cries and feel anything other than contempt. She doesn't deserve my pity, yet I can't help but feel bad for her. She's losing the only parent she has left.

'Here's a copy of your grandmother's will, if you'd like to read along,' Jonah says, handing me a large white envelope.

I don't bother opening it. I don't think I could handle seeing the words printed on paper.

An hour later, we walk out of Lynch & Mellman, LLC, with the knowledge that my grandmother left me all her assets and, not surprisingly, she does not want to be kept on life support. No one says a word, until we reach the parking lot and I speak directly to Joe.

'I don't know how much of this she'll remember later, so you need to be straight with her and make her read her copy of the will.'

'I know what's going on,' Elaine insists. I can't see her eyes through the dark sunglasses and she's hanging on to Joe's wrist like a lifeline. 'I ain't as stupid as you think. I understood that lawyer-talk. I know she's givin' you everything because she hates me. I ain't . . . I ain't stupid.'

I shake my head at this response. 'You're not going to make me feel guilty for the fact that Grandma trusted me more than you.' I turn back to Joe. 'When she's sober, tell her everything and make her read it, even if she says she remembers. And tell her I'll allow her to attend the funeral, but then make sure to tell her that I don't give a shit if she ends up homeless for the rest of her life. She's not getting a dime from Grandma or me, but . . . but if she wants the house, I'll pay for her to go to rehab. Once she's clean for a year, I'll give her the house – no strings attached – as long as she promises never to come looking for Molly or me. Is that clear?'

Joe raises his craggy eyebrows as if he's not impressed. 'You can't just forget your family.'

'She's not my family. Never has been.'

I walk away feeling lighter than I've felt for the past two days. I still have to go to the hospital and do the most difficult thing I've ever done in my life, but I can do it now knowing for certain that it was Grandma's last wish. And after all the wishes that came true for me because of her, this is the least I can do.

Chapter Thirty-Nine

We hold a small ceremony at the funeral home for Elaine to attend. Then we hold a private ceremony the next day where we bury Grandma's ashes on a frosty morning under an elm tree in the backyard of our house in Cary. It's January 5th. Chris and Claire and Jake and Rachel cut their honeymoons short so they could be here with us. Everyone heads inside to escape the cold, but Molly and I stay outside to spend just a little while longer with Grandma.

'We're not guaranteed anything good in this life, Molly, but Grandma was something good.' I stare at the pewter urn that holds what's left of the strongest woman I've ever known and I can't believe I didn't spend every waking moment of her final weeks with her since the diagnosis. 'We were lucky.'

Molly sniffs loudly and wipes at her face. 'I wish I felt lucky.'

'Yeah, me too.'

She grabs my forearm and the look on her face

breaks my heart. 'Sit with me for a while?' We sit on the cold, wet grass in silence for a few minutes before she speaks. 'Grandma told me . . . she told me she had a dream that Senia had a baby girl. I forgot about this until last night when I was going through my room and I saw the dream catcher she gave me last year. She told me that she knew when you were born that you were destined to be surrounded by pretty girls for the rest of your life.' She stuffs her hands in her coat pockets and smiles. 'I wish I'd told her that I'm not so pretty, just to get a smile out of her. I miss her smile already.'

This comment gives me an idea. Tonight, I'll ask Senia to help me create a photo book for Molly composed solely of pictures of her and Grandma smiling. Senia was so happy when she finally found the box of old photos she needed for her project. She told me last night about all the plans she has to keep Molly busy over the next few weeks: a tour of the UNC campus, dinner with Chris and Claire, a winter bonfire in Carolina Beach, just to name a few. I was surprised to find that Molly had no objections to any of Senia's suggestions.

'I have a pretty nice smile, too. Don't you agree?' I reply and she pushes me sideways.

'No, I don't agree.'

'Well, you're the only one, but you are kind of weird, so that makes sense.'

'Does Senia actually like it when you say stuff like that?'

'Senia loves it when I tell her she's weird.'

She pulls one of her hands out of her coat pocket and reaches forward to break off a blade of frosty grass. She holds it up in front of her face, tilting it up and down and side to side as she watches the microscopic droplets of dew catch the rays of morning light. 'You know what I'll miss more than her smile?'

'Her laugh?'

'Her music.'

Grandma Flo always put on music while she was cooking. Her favorite was Frank Sinatra, but she had a not-so-secret love for all things Katy Perry. One of the last songs she asked Molly to download onto her iPhone was 'Unconditionally.' I caught Grandma with her headphones on a couple of times, singing along to Katy as she scrolled through her newsfeed on Facebook. I think one of my biggest regrets will be that she never got to see me perform any of the songs on the new album.

Molly and I spend a little while longer, reminiscing about all the things we'll miss the most, then we head back inside. We haven't started packing yet. We still have ten days before Chris and I exchange homes. I'm not taking much with me, anyway. This house is huge and his condo barely has 1,700 square feet of living space. I'm only taking our beds, my instruments and equipment, and some personal items.

Molly heads straight for the slate fireplace in the living room to warm her hands as I head for the kitchen.

It's difficult not to reach for a beer or a bottle of vodka at a time like this, but I'm taking it one day at a time. I'm trying to be better, for Senia and Molly, and for the baby I never got to know.

From where she sits on a stool at the breakfast bar, Claire watches me as I enter the kitchen. Suddenly, she slides off the stool and throws her arms around me. I look to Chris and he shrugs as she continues to hold on. Finally, I lift my arms slowly and return the hug. A moment later, she lets go and wipes tears from her face as she walks out of the kitchen. Chris walks after her and I immediately look around for Senia. I find her sitting at the dining table with Rachel, both of them dabbing at their pink, puffy eyes.

I don't have to say a word. She stands from the table and follows me upstairs to the bedroom to lie down.

'She's just thinking of her mom,' Senia says as she lays her head on my shoulder, and I know she's referring to Claire.

'I know. I just wasn't expecting that.'

If there's anyone who knows how unfair it is that we can't choose our parents, it's Claire. I used to envy her. Her mom was a heroin addict like Elaine, but she didn't have to grow up with her mother the way I did. After her mother died, it took Claire a long time to find her way to Jackie's house. I had Grandma all these years, but I was still constantly faced with the reminder of the childhood I lost every time Elaine showed up at Grandma's and shit all over my day. Now, I realize that neither Claire nor I had it any easier. I got twenty-one years with Grandma and she only got seven years with her mom. Life isn't fair, to anyone.

But God damn if it doesn't always give us exactly what and who we need, exactly when we need them.

Chapter Forty

Senia walks through the front door of our new condo wearing a black knee-length trench coat and black boots that cover her knees. She shakes off her umbrella outside before she stuffs it in the umbrella stand just inside the door. When she looks up, her face is glowing with mischief.

'That lady stumbled all over herself apologizing.' She's talking about Carissa's mom who unfairly judged Molly that time Carissa got her drunk. 'I shared some phony memories of Grandma Flo with her – how she taught me to read and bake a pie, stuff like that. I hope that woman wallows in her guilt for at least a couple of days.'

I set down the bowl of cereal I just fixed for myself and try to figure out why she's so damn happy about this. Then it dawns on me.

The doctor told Senia and me that we had to wait two weeks after Senia lost the baby before we could have sex again. It's been an excruciating two weeks.

The first night, we tried very hard not to touch each other, but that didn't last. We ended up making out and feeling each other up for about five minutes before I finally told her I couldn't take it any more. We've spent the last two weeks making out like teenagers for hours in our bed and, well, the oral sex has been great, but it's not the same as being inside her. Nothing is as good as being inside her.

'It's been two weeks,' she declares as she walks toward me. 'Molly is away for the weekend. The wait is over.'

I clasp my hand around the back of her neck and pull her toward me. Her lips are soft and cool from being outside. I kiss her hungrily and she gives me a soft *mmm* sound, which gets me even hotter.

'You ready to try out that steam room?'

'This condo doesn't have a steam room. Besides, I'd rather steam up *this* room.'

She grabs the front of my shirt and drags me out of the kitchen, around the breakfast bar, and toward the dining table. She pulls out a dining chair and makes me sit on it backwards, so my chest is facing the back of the chair. Then she strips her coat off, slowly undoing each button, and I'm not surprised to see that she's stark naked underneath except for a pair of black knee-high tights. She slips her boots off and I feel the excitement and longing growing with my erection. I hastily pull my wallet out of my back pocket and toss it aside once I have a condom in hand. She smiles as

I undo my jeans and slide it on, then she climbs onto my lap.

I groan as she lowers herself onto me. 'Fuck, yes.'

Cradling her face in my hands, I kiss her slowly and try to focus on her mouth instead of the pleasure of being wrapped inside her. I don't want to come too quickly. Thankfully, she moves slowly up and down the length of my cock, completely stopping when she feels I'm getting close.

I slide my hand between us to reach her clit and she throws her head back. I suck on the column of her throat, savoring the vibration of her moans as they tickle my lips. If it weren't for this condom, I would have exploded by now. Even so, I wrap my arm tightly around her waist and hold her still so I can just caress her for a bit.

'You're so beautiful,' I whisper against her skin and she whimpers as she gets closer to orgasm. I remove my hand from between her legs and lift her off my lap. 'Get up. I don't want to come yet.'

She stands and I sit there admiring her body for a moment. Her round breasts and curvy hips look practically edible. And the fucking knee-highs!

'Put one foot on the chair.'

She smiles as she lifts her leg and points her toe as she sets it down on the seat of the chair. I kneel before her and slide my fingers inside her to unearth her wetness. She places one hand on the back of the chair while her other hand clutches my hair for support. I massage her a little until I think she's close to climax, then I part her flesh and take her clit into my mouth.

'Oh God,' she breathes, her body trembling as I lovingly massage and suck her clit as if it were my only source of lifeblood. For me, it is.

Her legs begin to weaken as she comes and I keep one arm wrapped firmly around her thigh and the other around her waist to hold her steady. She screams my name so loudly, I nearly come at the sound of it. I quickly stand up, completely unable to hold back this urge any longer. I lift her off the ground and she deftly wraps her legs around my hips. I pin her against the wall and let out a rapturous moan as I sink into her.

'I love you,' I whisper in her ear, burying my face in her neck. 'I love you so fucking much.'

'I love you more.'

I don't say *I love you most* because I don't argue with Senia. There's no sense in arguing with her. She always wins. But as I come harder than I've ever come, I can't help but feel like I'm the one who won today.

Our bodies are sticky with sweat as I carry her to the bedroom. I lay a few soft kisses on her shoulder as I walk and she clutches a fistful of my hair as she attempts to catch her breath. When I lay her down on the bed, I laugh as she yanks me down on top of her and wraps her arms and legs tightly around me.

'Don't leave.'

I kiss her temple and nuzzle my nose against her ear. 'I won't.'

One. Two. Three.

I was twelve years old and it was just three weeks.

One. Two. Three.

Grandma. Molly. Me.

One. Two. Three.

Senia. Me. The baby.

One. Two. Three.

Grandma Flo's radiant face materializes at my side. It's my ninth birthday and the smell of cake is sweet in the air. She leans in and whispers in my ear, 'Count to three and make a wish.'

Looking down at Senia where she's fallen asleep next to me, hugging my arm like a teddy bear, my only wish is that the ones I love never feel the need to abandon hope.

Epilogue

Four and a Half Years Later

Late August in Cary is a sight to behold. Emerald-green grass and trees as far as the eye can see. This is one of the things I missed after leaving my house in Cary. But Senia and I enjoyed the life we created in Chapel Hill: going out for the occasional beer with the rest of the gang when they weren't busy having kids or traveling. When they weren't around, Senia and I got very good at pretending to know what the heck we were doing with Molly. Maybe we did know what we were doing because she's still living with us – in our new house in North Raleigh – even though she started classes at UNC last week.

But it's no surprise that she didn't feel like coming to a birthday party for a four-year-old. She has to draw the line somewhere. As I pull our car into Chris and Claire's curved driveway, I can't help but feel a bit nostalgic for the brief time Molly spent here with Senia and me. The three of us have made a pretty great team and sometimes it's hard to remember that she's not my daughter – especially since I never heard from Elaine again after Grandma's funeral. I wish I could say I worry about Elaine, but I don't.

The crying begins just as I kill the engine. 'She's calling your name,' I say to Senia as I open the car door.

'She's two months old,' she replies as she slides out of the passenger seat and immediately opens the door to the backseat. 'If she's able to call either of our names, it has to be yours, Da-Da.'

'Very funny.'

Senia caught me trying to teach Sia – short for Florencia – how to say Da-Da the other day. I'm not stupid. I know she can't speak yet, but there's no harm in hammering it into her head. Da-Da *will* be the first word she says.

She takes Sia out of the car seat and I grab the baby bag from the trunk. I can't help but reach for her feather-soft cheeks as we walk toward Chris and Claire's front door. I wish I could touch those cheeks all day long.

Senia doesn't bother knocking or ringing the doorbell; she just walks right in. Old habits die hard and Chris and Claire are family so it makes no sense to knock here. Besides, I work here and they're all probably out in the backyard celebrating Jimi's fourth birthday already. We're a little late to the party today because Senia wouldn't leave until Molly understood the concept of standard deviation. I'm glad someone in this family understands statistics.

I don't know much about anything other than music, which is why, when I decided to quit touring, I expanded the small music studio I originally installed in this house – with Chris and Claire's permission. We now record all our albums here in Cary, but when it's time to tour, Chris and Jake take Will Rawlings in my place. I know Grandma would be proud to know that I never abandoned my family when they needed me.

Jake spots us first as we walk through the back doors out onto the patio. It's a small party for a few family and friends, so I should have no problems executing my plans for later today. I just need to make sure Chris and Claire do their part.

'Hey, man,' Jake says, giving me a one-armed bro-hug.

Rachel kisses both Senia and me on the cheek, then she gazes longingly at Sia. 'Can I hold her?'

'Of course,' Senia replies as she hands over my precious girl.

Rachel wanted to wait until the touring slowed down before she and Jake had kids. They were all set to start trying for a baby next year, until Rachel developed PCOS – polycystic ovary syndrome. Now, she's not sure she wants to take the risk of having a miscarriage.

I've tried to get Senia to talk to her about it, but Senia still has a little bit of a problem talking about the baby we lost. There's something that happens when you lose a child, no matter what stage of their development. The experience definitely made us appreciate what Chris and Claire struggle with every day. I just hope that one day, the hole in Senia's heart will close a little bit more. And I hope that Rachel and Jake will get the chance to feel what I feel every day with my Sia. Like a part of my soul that died a long time ago was reanimated, given a second chance.

Rachel and Senia wander off to deal with the kids and to show Sia off to all the other parents. Jake turns to me with a serious expression. 'I got what you asked me to get,' he mutters out the side of his mouth. 'It's in the freezer.'

'Thanks, man.'

We set off to find Chris. I need to make sure he and Claire came through with their roles in today's surprise. On the way to the kids' play area, I'm stopped by Joel, Jackie's new husband. He could be Jake's dad with that lumberjack beard.

He claps me on the arm. 'Where's your wife and baby? We got something for the baby.'

'She's not my wife, but she's right over there,' I say, nodding toward the patio area where Claire, Rachel, and Senia are fawning over Sia.

'Well, you should get on that. Girls like her don't come along but once in a blue moon.'

I sigh at this advice. Joel is a great guy, but he's become quite comfortable with telling me I need to hurry up and get married. He doesn't know that Senia is the one who has refused to marry me. I've asked her to marry me twice and both times she shot me down. The first time she told me she wanted to finish school before she started worrying about planning a wedding. I asked her again the day she graduated from UNC – I'm nothing if not completely compulsive and eager when it comes to Senia. She still turned me down. She didn't want me to just ask her because 'it was time.' She wanted me to ask her when the time was right. She said I'd know when that time came. And she was right – as she always is.

It seemed logical that I should ask her as soon as we found out she was pregnant last year, but I didn't. I knew she wouldn't want to look back on her wedding pictures and remember that she was two months or six months pregnant. I knew she would want to wait. So I've waited patiently for the past ten months, biding my time and making my plans. I don't know what she's going to say, but I hope to God that I've planned it right this time.

After the birthday cake is cut, I walk inside the house to begin putting the plan in motion. If everything is going as planned out there, Claire should be offering to take Sia while Senia goes to look for me. I can just imagine Senia's face when Claire tells her that we're going to play hide-and-seek.

I open the freezer and retrieve the surprise that Jake brought for us, then I reach into my pocket and retrieve the ring that Chris just handed to me behind the bouncer. Now, I just have to get to my hiding place before Senia gets there.

Once I'm settled into the darkness of my hiding spot, I close my eyes, trying to keep calm, as I wait for her. She's going to say yes. She has to.

She'd *better* say yes or I'm going to ravage her tonight. She'd like that.

The door handle turns and the sound of Senia's laughter is like music to my ears. A crack of light appears, just enough for me to see my surroundings and I quickly rise from the bench and turn on the light switch. Senia opens the door all the way and shakes her head when she sees me standing in the steam room, holding a bowl of frozen yogurt, with a ring sitting on top like a three-carat cherry on the life we've built.

She presses her lips together as I take her hand and pull her into the steam room. 'Yes,' she says with a nod. 'Just . . . yes.'

I scoop the ring out of the yogurt and she smiles as I lick it clean then I slide it onto her finger. I plant a soft kiss on the back of her hand, then I kiss her madly.

'If you didn't say yes this time,' I whisper in her ear, 'I was going to break out the whips tonight.'

'In that case, no.'

I kiss her again and a million thoughts race through my mind, but the one that stands out amongst them all is this: *You can't let your past define your future*. Once you get that figured out, you begin to understand the joy of living in the present. And the present is full of tiny gifts that we can only see when we stop looking behind and ahead of us. Sometimes, these gifts land right at our feet. Sometimes, it's our feet that carry us toward them, running at full speed until our hearts nearly give out. Either way, never stop noticing them, and never stop wishing.

Take a sneak peek at the
heartwrenching stand-alone novel
by Cassia Leo

BLACK BOX

Chapter One

January 8th

Mikki

The moment you realize you're going to die is nothing like I imagined it would be. I imagined a deep internal struggle coupled with a visceral, physical response – fight or flight. But there's no fighting this. I'm going to die.

It's possible that everyone on this plane is going to die. I wonder if they feel this overwhelming sense of peace, or if the squeal of the plane engine has drowned out all their thoughts.

He grabs the oxygen mask as it drops from the compartment and he's yelling something as he puts the elastic band over my head. He pulls his own mask over his head then he grabs my hand and looks me in the eye. There's no panic in his eyes. Maybe he feels this same calm I'm feeling. Or maybe he just wants me to know that he loves me.

He loves me.

Or maybe the look in his eyes is his way of telling me he trusts that whatever happens to us in the next few seconds was meant to be.

Fate.

I used to think fate was for religious nuts and people who were too afraid to take their fate into their own hands. Now I know the truth.